Praise for Gnarly Wounds

"In the tradition of forebears Borges and Angela Carter comes a complex and wonderful puzzle named *Gnarly Wounds*. It has humor, intrigue, violence, love, talking animals, a social conscience, and the most important ingredient of all, humanness."

—Joshua Mohr, author of *Fight Song, Damascus, Termite Parade,* and *Some Things That Meant the World to Me.*

GNARLY

WOUNDS

A Comic Mystery In Three Parts

JAYSON IWEN

Emergency Press
New York

For information about permissions to reproduce selections from this book, translation rights, or to order bulk purchases, write to Emergency Press at info@emergencypress.org.

Design by Lindsay Gatz/Artsy Geek

Iwen, Jayson
Gnarly Wounds: A Comic Mystery in Three Parts
ISBN 978-0-9885694-1-6
1. Fiction—Literary. 2. Fiction—General.

Emergency Press
154 W. 27th St.
#5W
New York NY 10001
emergencypress.org

Printed in the United States of America
Distributed by Publishers Group West

for America

"First of all, I do not see any inherent contradiction between the imaginary and reality. To distinguish, in the case of myths, between the 'true' and the 'untrue' is the wrong way of looking at the problem. Myth presupposes a certain structure, and it matters little, fundamentally, whether this structure incorporates material which is true or fictive, or a combination of the two. All that is important is that it arranges it according to the logic of the imaginary."

—Lucian Boia, *History and Myth in Romanian Consciousness*

"A joke, on the other hand, is the most social of all the mental functions that aim at a yield of pleasure. It often calls for three persons and its completion requires the participation of someone else in the mental process it starts. The condition of intelligibility is, therefore, binding on it; it may only make use of possible distortion in the unconscious through condensation and displacement up to the point at which it can be set straight by the third person's understanding […] the joke will evade restrictions and open sources of pleasure that have become inaccessible."

—Sigmund Freud, *Jokes and Their Relation to the Unconscious*

"Our laughter was hard. We used it to drill into our pain."

—Herta Müller, *Herztier*

Editor's Note

On a sticky, Midwestern, midsummer morning, I found a box containing a one-thousand-and-forty-nine-page manuscript on the floor before my apartment door. The title page of the manuscript identified it as *Gnarly Wounds*, purportedly written by one "Nicholaus Iwinski," and translated by one "Ronald Ionescu," which, upon further reflection, I remembered was the name of a man living down the hall from me. The post-it note affixed to the title page read, "Mr. Iwen, please look after this for me while I'm gone. Should there be a fire, please take it with you. I'll be back soon." Fifteen years later, it's still in my apprehensive possession.

Of Nicholaus Iwinski I know only what Ionescu has written of him in the translator's note that accompanied the manuscript. As any good editor would, I did my research and discovered that this Iwinski character seems to have left no trace on history. Incidentally, regarding the bizarre factual, spatial, and chronological incongruities you will no doubt encounter, I would simply like it to be noted that I attempted to execute my editorial duty to the fullest extent possible. However, in such matters the publisher claimed final authority, and chose to "retain idiosyncrasies for the sake of artifactual authenticity."

Regarding the character of Ronald Ionescu, I know little more than that I would occasionally encounter him in the byways of our apartment building weekday evenings, on my way home from work at the newspaper. He was perhaps the most humorless and reticent man I've ever had the pleasure of meeting. Despite several attempts on my part, I was unable to engage him in a proper conversation. He never invited me over, so I never returned the courtesy. Despite occasional moaning, he was a quiet neighbor.

Of his appearance, the only details I remember are that he was a thin, grey Caucasian male, in a perpetually wrinkled suit and tie, who somehow managed to appear as if it had always been a couple days since he'd shaven. Though I have since been informed his eyes were green, as I told the police, I can't recall having noticed their color. I recall a look of restrained wildness in them, but not the particular color of that wildness. I suppose green would have been appropriate. To my knowledge he was a retired banker of some sort. Anne, the gossip across the hall, was more successful at extracting the spoken word from him, and has told me he moved to Milwaukee from some little town up north after his wife died. I believe she said something about a daughter, in some sort of band, who'd also gone missing. I haven't been able to verify these particulars with anyone else in the building, and the police haven't shared their findings. He was there when I moved in, and he was gone when I left. That's all I know for sure. And I don't plan to investigate further. We all have our own lives to live, and, besides, that's what cops are for. That's why we pay taxes. Editing this book was enough involvement for me.

You may have noticed by now that the book before you is not one-thousand-and-forty-nine-pages in length. Though I suspect the publisher suffers an unhealthy fascination with this whole affair, he seems to be exercising fiscal restraint, and has asked that I select only the "gnarliest of the wounds." Therefore, what you hold is a mere fraction of the original manuscript. The fruit of my throbbing eyes. Perhaps, if critics find it to be the work of genius Ionescu claims it to be, or if there's an irrational demand from the masses of less discriminating consumers, the other seventy percent might be made public some day.

Jayson Iwen
Milwaukee, 2012

Translator's Note

At the onset of World War II, Nicholaus Iwinski's parents fled from Warsaw to Bucharest, where his maternal grandparents lived. Nicholaus was born in the year 1943. By the age of twenty-two he had already become one of the country's leading humorists, and had secured a position writing columns for the Romanian branch of *Pravda*. His earlier work satirized Capitalism, Christianity, and Romanian folklore, but by 1967 he had turned the barb of his wit upon the Council of State, and, in particular, its newly elected president, Nicolae Ceausescu. He lost his job that year. In 1968, when he tried to start his own press in the basement of his parents' house, Securitate officers burned the house down, with his parents inside, and relocated Iwinski to a "reeducation center" in the Transylvanian Alps. He was kept there for three years, after which the authorities declared him sane, and he was sent back to Bucharest.

Upon his release, Iwinski was assigned a position as a municipal garbage collector. This he did during the day, and nightly he worked feverishly at Gnarly Wounds in his single-room housing unit. How he managed to conceal his labor from the authorities is unknown. Likewise, how the book was finally printed and distributed is a maddeningly elusive mystery. But, on the frigid morning of February 7th, 1974, it is said there was a copy on nearly every doorstep in Bucharest. By direct order of Nicolae Ceausescu, the Securitate confiscated all copies they could find. By noon they had located Iwinski midway through his garbage route and arrested him. After fifteen hours of torture and interrogation, Iwinski was strangled to death. His body was then transported to University Square, where it was cremated on a great pyre of the books which Securitate officers had confiscated. All other evidence of his existence was subsequently erased, by order of the President.

It is currently rumored that three copies of *Gnarly Wounds* survived this macabre conflagration. One fell into my hands shortly after my wife and daughter departed. It came to me by way of a Canadian business associate who was in Romania from 1990 to 1992, working for the World Bank as an economic advisor for new Romanian capital ventures. Another copy is reported to have fallen into the hands of Yoshio Iwasaki, an associate professor of Soviet Studies at Kyoto University, who was translating the collected works of Iwinski into Japanese. Iwasaki hung himself in 1989, but, tragically, not before burning all his unpublished writings in a fit of despair, including any work he may have done on *Gnarly Wounds*. His copy of the original text was never found. Likewise, the location of the third existing copy has never been revealed, not even in the inner-most circle of Iwinski scholars.

So you, dear reader, now hold in *your* hands the only version of this text that is officially known to exist in any language. Hopefully, you too will recognize the genius that was necessary to lift the mundane and vulgar genre of the comic to the sublime level Iwinski has achieved in *Gnarly Wounds*. Certainly, the historical significance of the text will be lost on no one.

Ronald Ionescu
Milwaukee, 1997

GNARLY WOUNDS

HELL'S CANARY

On a personal tour of Bucharest University, Nicolae Ceausescu visits the restroom. His bodyguards clear the room of all occupants, including a psychologist whose pants are still about his ankles when he's thrown from the room. Ceausescu then enters. His bodyguards stand outside with their backs to the door.

Ceausescu begins by appraising the reported graffiti. Eventually, he finds something he likes and undoes his pants. He unpeels his bikini underwear a bit, and beats off for twenty minutes or so before the tiny, strangely enticing statement, "It's dark in mama's ass," which he finds inscribed on the grout between the tiles above a urinal. He then finds a stall he likes and sits, with profound resignation, on the toilet. On the back of the stall door is written, "Hung(a)ry? Call 1 800 EAT MAMA." This pleases him.

After a most relieving dump, which rolls his eyes back, bites his lip, and smells like the fields of his youth, Nicolae rinses his hands in a healthy stream of his own urine and orders a bodyguard to set up the satellite phone. He dials the number. "Mama," he says, "have we gotten any calls yet?"

"Just you," Elena says, "my big furry bear."

What do you get when you cross space and time? When you cross an author with his subject? Say, the dictator's drunken son Nicu with the twelve-year-old daughter of a government functionary?

Answer: Another pair of panties, these ones white, speckled with dainty blue flowers, hanging on a hook in the fuck chamber. And a boy child his mother dies giving birth to. We'll call him Nicu Junior, or Nicu for short. You get Nicu again. You get confused, but it's okay. Confusion is natural at this point. Souls float from vessel to vessel, from time to time. The Ceausescus themselves adopt the child and keep him hidden in one of their summer homes, the lake castle of Vlad Tepes, in the care of three of Nicolae's concubines-cum-wet nurses. They never reveal to Nicu his true origins, nor allow him to meet his biological father, in the event that the real Nicu will need a stunt double some day. They too become confused, and send the wrong one to the mountains when things start heating up.

Why did I cross the threshold with Ceausescu in my arms?

Answer: To get to the other side.

When he's fifteen, Nicolae and Elena send Nicu to a monastery high in the Transylvanian Alps, to be trained by Rana the Wise. He can take nothing with him, and has to live just as the monks do, until the Securitate hunts down the "foreign agitators" and restores order to the country.

On the first day of his training, Nicu sits with Rana at the edge of a cliff, beneath a gnarled willow. Rana sits with his eyes closed and says nothing. Nicu looks into the valley below and scratches himself.

"These robes itch," he says.

Rana says nothing.

"Rana, why must fighting be a part of our philosophy," Nicu says.

"Never address me as Rana," Rana says, his eyes still closed. "To you I am Master, until you die."

Nicu sighs. "Master, why must I learn how to hurt others? In Paris, professors don't teach students how to punch each other."

Rana opens his eyes and squints at Nicu. "We must know how to touch others and what it means for them to touch us," he says. "Tell me, are we one or are we many?"

"I don't know," says Nicu.

"If we are one, why are we surprised when our touching hurts?" Rana then punches Nicu in the nose, quick as a lizard, and Nicu sings out in surprise, and blood springs forth, and Nicu tries to stop it by pinching the bridge of his nose.

"There is no mind separate from body," Rana says. "There is no East or West. There is no kindness or selfishness. There is only blood and singing. Remember that. Now, let us eat, for there is hunger too, and I am fucking starving."

A military hospital in Timisoara, shortly after the massacre. A nurse enters a ward where five soldiers lie wounded: a Wallachian Gypsy, a Moldavian Jew, two Transylvanian Hungarians, and an asshole.

"Who buzzed this body and soul," says the nurse.

"Which is body and which is soul," says Soldier Three.

"The same as the ones that were here when last she was," says Soldier One.

"I'm not them," she says.

"You're the same," says One.

"Are we," she asks.

"Who's 'we' when she says it alone," asks Three.

"All of us in this room are we when we're here," says One.

"And when I'm not," asks the nurse, "am I not we, when I'm gone, before you buzz and after I leave?"

"I'm your body," says One.

"Can I be her soul," asks Three.

"I'm her cat," says Two.

"I'm her memory," says One.

"I'm your childhood crush," says Two.

"Help," says Soldier Five. "I'm dying."

"I'm your last summer," says Three.

"I'm what you decided never to do again," says One.

"Then who am I," asks she.

"She's never gone," says Three.

"Then why do we have to buzz her," says Two.

"We're always here when we're here together," says One.

"Then who am I when I'm gone," she asks.

"We don't know," says Two, "and by we I mean you."

A doctor enters and speaks. "Who keeps buzzing," he says. "Nurse, help these men with their belongings." He turns to the men. "You're all better now. Pack up and leave. We need to make more room for the civilians."

All leave, but Soldier Five who lies still 'til the curtain falls.

———————————

A Jew, an Arab, and a young political whore named Nicolae Ceausescu are stranded on a desert island.

"What's your greatest fear," the Arab asks the Jew.

"This," the Jew replies.

"And what's yours," the Arab asks Ceausescu.

"I'm most afraid of what I might become before I die," he says. "It's not death, you see, that terrifies me. It's how I might prove myself either too constant or too variable to tolerate. I suppose this means I am afraid of the rigidity of my own expectations, that either they will turn me into an automaton or I will shatter them, and with them I will shatter. That's what I'm afraid of, that I will go mad one day, that, in fact, I am already mad and it is only the stability of my present madness that conceals itself from me. It is only the stability of my current madness that makes my future madness so flagrant. I dream the dream of the state."

"So," says the Arab, "I'm randy as shit. Who's the professional whore around here?"

———————

How may X's does it take to recognize that X is the destination of all their effort?

Answer: X

———————

Nicu is trying to explain to his parents why he feels he has to leave home, when he is suddenly struck by the overwhelming feeling that he is related to no other human being on the face of the earth. He doesn't know who these people are, or why he's speaking to them. It's as if he has descended to the earth in a deep-sea diving suit, and a crease in his air hose has suddenly reminded him of this. Their mouths are moving, but all he can hear is the celestial hum of the bottom of the sea. A transparent fish swims past. He's running out of air, but his suit is too heavy for him to swim to the surface, and he's lost communication with the people up top, and it strikes him that soon he will have to learn to breathe water.

———————

A humorist, chained to a wall in a sound-proof cell, is visited by his reeducation officer.

The officer begins: "When you left everyone else's world, you appeared in mine, and I don't give a shit who or what you thought you were before you appeared in my world. There's only my world now. And I want you to know that if you're a good boy, and if I decide some day to allow you to physically leave here, you will not be returning to the world you left behind. At that point, you will simply be stepping into a larger version of my world. Just as I'm telling you there is no other world now, there will have never been another world that you could have possibly imagined then. And you will know it for yourself. In other words, from now on, your mind is here for good. Your life will be a dream you dream from this room. You are about to be reborn out of nothing, and I am going to be your mother and father and midwife and best friend and lover and anyone who has ever been, or ever will be, anything to you. Is that clear?"

Humorist: "When the eyes of the flesh are shut, the eyes of the spirit are open."

"That's good," the officer says. "Who said that?"

"She's a place where he can cool off," says the humorist.

"Alright," says the officer, "have it your way." He takes a pair of latex gloves from his pocket and starts putting them on. "Are you allergic to latex," he asks.

"Imagine them there beyond hatred, falling asleep in the afternoon sun," says the humorist.

"Alright," says the officer, "here we go."

————————

Three witches, wearing black cloaks, stand around a cauldron in the dark of a sycamore grove.

"Lend me some tongues of babes, will you," says Witch One to Witch Two.

"Will three do?"

"Should."

"Here you go."

"Oh, I like these. How do you keep them so soft?"

"Piss."

"Elegantly simple."

One tosses them into the cauldron. "Yep, that did it," she says. "Reception's improving."

"What do you see," asks Witch Three.

"I see three men taking turns writing a book. When one takes a break, another sits down in his place and continues. But everything the new man writes is an act of revenge upon his predecessor. And, since they write in rotation, each man is eventually his own predecessor."

"I like the sound of it," says Two.

"Yes, it suits my disposition as well," says One.

"From the tongues of babes."

"Hallelujah."

After retreating, Soldiers One, Three, and Four regroup on a cliff overlooking Targu Jiu.

"Where's the rest of the unit," asks Three.

"I don't know," says One. "But I do know we've lost the town and we've no shelter now. We lay our heads with the wolves and the stars tonight."

"What will they do to the villagers? To my sweet potato?"

"Just what you did to her when we took the city. Don't worry. She'll ingratiate herself with her new master, and survive as she did before. Look how the fires on the plain bleed into the sunset's fury."

"Is that singing or crying I hear?"

Soldier Two joins them. He could be panting or weeping. "My sister's son fell as we were retreating," he says. "I heard him cry out and I turned. A Turk had struck him from behind, and he fell and wasn't moving. His golden tresses glowing with blood. I split the Turk's skull from crown to jaw and took the boy in my arms. 'Tell mother I'm sorry,' he said. Oh God, to hear him call my sister 'mother' in a voice like my own, and to hear her tell me again and again to take care of her headstrong son. I couldn't carry him. I couldn't."

He stares silently ahead.

"You're bleeding," says One.

———————

Nicu walks into a bar and says, "The only waste of time is eternity. Give me a scotch on the rocks."

"Blah blah blah," says the bartender, "beauty death beauty."

"How can you stand there and say that?" says Nicu. "To make a life out of living. You make me sick."

"Blah blah blah," says the bartender, "up the purple party dress of night, up her…"

"Stop right there," says Nicu. "Don't make my heart ache to ecstasy."

"Blah blah blah," says the bartender, "unzipping my shroud. Not a star but a star. Blah fucking blah blah blah."

Nicu drinks to that.

———————

A joke is being beaten. A joke is fucking itself. Two men fuck each other with a joke. Or, more accurately, each man's mother fucks the other man with her son's tongue.

———————

Ceausescu takes Arafat on a tour of his trophy hunting collection. He pauses before a bear standing perfectly upright, its gaze cast perfectly downward, and its front paws hanging dejectedly at its sides. Arafat glances quickly between Ceausescu and the bear, appreciating the intimacy and virility of the moment, yet still irritated by this decidedly unrevolutionary delay in his schedule. Ceausescu places his arm around Arafat's shoulders and speaks:

"Here he stands taller than he did in life,
My last poacher. Your eyes are knives,
My fedayeen. Slide them in between
The teeth, and you will see what seems
To be a second, smaller set of teeth.
Plunge them into the eyes of the beast,
And what do you see? Yes, now you see it.
I can see it on your face. Not unlike
The expression on his when we apprehended him
Field-dressing this most Dacian
Of ursines, which, by divine right, is mine.
Lucian brought me my Glenlivet
And an easy chair from which to watch him finish,
And when he had, I asked him to skin it,
A task he dispatched with such facility
My spirit rose inside of me,
Cupped its hands about my inner ear,
And through me bade him, 'don the bear.'
'On all fours,' I said. 'Be the bear.
That's it! Yes! Fill me with fear!'
And while he fortified my soul with grunts
Lucian handed me my gun.
'Now,' I commanded, 'advance upon me,
Ye who hath possessed the soul of the beast!'
And here, in the pose he then assumed, he stands
Preserved by Mihai's skillful hand.
Yes, you see, through the eyes of the beast, the man.
Now, here's my favorite, a stuffed Parisian."

Arafat can't hold it any longer, and looses an eerie, otherworldly fart.

"My God," says Ceausescu, "did you hear that? I've never heard anything as beautiful in all my life."

At night, four soldiers sneak back into Targoviste, a town their army lost to the enemy the previous day, so that Two might steal his girlfriend back. At the edge of town they encounter an enemy soldier who has snuck away from his unit to pillage with impunity. They surround him in a ramshackle house, and all are now whispering as loudly as possible.

"Surrender yourself," says One.

"Fuck off," says the enemy soldier. "God is on my side!"

"What?" says Two. "How could God be on your side?"

"I saw a sign this morning! An owl landed on the barrel of my gun!"

"We have you surrounded," says One. "Isn't that a sign?"

"That's an artificial sign! I'm talking about natural signs!"

Soldier Four, staring at an overturned wheelbarrow, says nothing.

"So we're not part of nature," says Two.

"No! You have free will!"

"And the owl didn't have free will," asks One.

"No! It was an agent of God's will!"

"And God doesn't have free will," asks One.

"No! I mean Yes! God is the only thing that does!"

"And man," says Soldier Three. "You said man has free will too!"

"Yes! God and man, his experiment!"

"Shut up," One hisses at Three. "We're trying to confuse him."

Two continues. "But if God has free will, and God was acting through the owl, then the owl had free will through God!"

"No!"

"Why not?"

"It doesn't work that way!"

"Couldn't the owl have been a sign that we're going to kick your ass," shouts One.

Enemy, to the owl sitting on his shoulder: "I hadn't thought of that."

At breakfast one morning, Nicu drops his bowl of cold oat gruel on the floor. Rana looks at him calmly and asks why he dropped the bowl.

"There was condensation on the bowl, and it was hard to grasp," says Nicu.

"That is true," says Rana, "but why did you drop the bowl?"

"I was thinking of the girl I left back in Bucharest," says Nicu, "and I forgot that I was holding my food."

"That is true," says Rana, "but why did you drop the bowl?"

"My fingers are dead because you made me carry buckets of water up the mountain all morning, and I couldn't hold the bowl."

"That is true," says Rana, "but why did you drop the bowl?"

"I forgot how hungry I was," Nicu yells. "I'm asleep now because the howling of wolves kept me up all night! I shook because you looked at me! I don't know!"

"You fill the emptiness with good reason," says Rana, "but why did you drop the bowl?"

"I really don't know what you're getting at," says Nicu, nervously.

"Why?"

Nicu screams and runs from the room.

"Very good," says Rana, "that'll teach the little shit."

Being in love is like…

Soldier Two: Stepping on a land mine filled with warm pudding.

Soldier One: Trading your car for a horse.

———————————

What is the voice that uses you, that bodies forth its song through you? What voice are you that questions use (when vomiting a lover cries this endless betrayal you call your past, the death that body makes for this)? What voice are you that anguish speaks? What voice is dirt when down you sing? Joy?

Answer: The voice is hydrogen fucking itself as long and slow as forever if it can. The voice that spoke you into being when it said I'm so sad I want to die, and I don't know why.

———————————

What is the purpose of a joke?

Answer A: Short-circuit psychic tension, unify disparities, engage in playful judgment, make sense of nonsense, engender enlightenment through bewilderment, unhide the hidden, and be brief.

Answer B: Get fucked up.

———————————

Nicu loses his wristwatch at some point in the evening. To find it, he retraces his steps in his mind. He walks to the tavern, to his stool, to the pissoir, to his stool, to the pissoir, to his stool, to the tree in the park, and back to his housing unit. He stands in the center of the room and slowly turns, taking everything in. He pauses when he gets to the picture of the martyrs of Timisoara. He looks down and sees himself lying in bed, and wakes with a start and looks around consciously, and there it is!

Four soldiers overwhelm their enemy with logic. They tie him up with a jump-rope and throw him into the basement. Now they're making themselves at home. Soldier One is standing naked in the bathtub when he yells through the open doorway, "Hey! Did I just take a bath or am I about to?"

"Don't know," yells back Two, "but it's better to take two than none at all."

"Good point," One yells back, "do I have time for a bath now?"

"I'll go up to the roof and see if they've started moving yet," yells Two.

Halfway up the stairs, Two stops and turns around. "Hey," he yells down, "was I going up the stairs or down?"

Three, observing the goings-on, says to Four, "Jesus, I hope I never get as forgetful as those two," and he knocks on wood, immediately after which he looks startled and calls out, "Come in!"

The front door swings open. Standing in the doorway is the enemy soldier, bruised and bloodied and visibly agitated. The rest of his unit is waiting in the front yard.

"How's this for a sign," he says, and clubs Three over the head with the butt of his pistol.

"Now I remember," says Two.

"Hey," yells One, "who shit in my bath water?"

What happens to a young woman who doesn't think the way the State tells her she should think, whose mind turns morbidly inward on itself to figure out what's wrong? What is *it* she doesn't understand? The *it* that becomes that thing: the *it* you won't allow yourself to have when she has left, when you travel far away from her and say to yourself, I will not have it until I am returned from afar. What is it she takes forever with her when she forever goes away? Even though it is always only yours to give yourself. And where is it that you've gone anyway?

Answer: Nicu comes home one night, when he's living with the love of his life, a perpetually sad woman named Ana. He has just taken his coat off when the report of a gunshot from the bedroom makes him to drop his coat to the floor. He runs to the bedroom and finds Ana sprawled across the bed with his service revolver in her hand. A sanguine spring arcing from the crown of her head. She isn't quite dead yet. While Nicu tries ineffectually to stem the flow by clamping his hand over her head, she makes a series of infantile sounds and blinks at him. He's crying now. And chanting, *No, No, No!* He tells her he loves her, he loves her more than life. She blinks a couple more times and stares in endless exasperation at his grief.

———————————

It must always return to these pages. For example, Soldier Four sits in a wheelchair beneath a flowering linden tree. Blossoms fall about him.

"Don't tell the others," he says. "They don't know I can speak. After we return to our homelands, there's one there who notices me. He's able to ease the words from me. But when he's had his fill, he leaves, and the love he leaves leaves me at the edge of this cliff. Now my legs have been amputated. Every time, it takes a part of me, but I think if I ever fall again I will succeed.

"Ah," *it* says, "I am pleased to hear you, and yes, next time love will get you right." And it shakes the highest branches, and the young man cries in the fragrance of the downfall. And it's just this kind of outburst that prevents him from speaking.

───────────

Having had, he went away to have a smoke under the trees under snow she sat up and went out too, when it was the old love her body slid from the frame and she thought, what are we thinking?

Answer: It walks into a bar with me and needs me to stay there all night long talking to it.

───────────

What is a body?

Answer: A body is a lot of thought. And two bodies talking is a thought rethinking itself. And a falling body is a thought recognizing itself. And a dead body is thinking that has come to a conclusion. What an offal idea is viscera-thought tossed to heaven. From fall springs the hot nothing of winter.

───────────

A Securitate officer pulls a humorist over.
    Officer: "Look lakeward. The vapor-fazed rolls in, in blinding sunlight, and chasmic makes, like ruin, the high-rises. Makes like tomorrow the past of my human-ness. Where's your wife?"
    Humorist: "Do all your kind speak like you? Everything either so beautiful or so hideous I want to die. And then with you I do."
    Officer: "No, I'm a motorcycle cop. We ride alone. What think you I? Like-you but unlike, in likeness of you-and-I. One says do

you all speak and one speaks. Nothing, not ever nothing, is simple for me. My nightstick in your blind-spot is no matter of any less than every silver-scale wave at daybreak. You say you die in me, but where is your wife? Has she too? In one that out lives the mother-hand. Please observe the signs."

Humorist: "An incomplete sadness in your signs."

Officer: "There are miles between. Please observe. The chromatic tonnage of sunset."

Why is there a paper silhouette of a bird taped to the window through which I gaze?

Answer: And then I met Ana. She said, "You must treat life like an animal, and use every part. Fish hooks from bones and babies do grow. No matter where you are, you must use it all. Every part of the animal. We live in a thought we cannot go beyond. The gazing becomes us. And the State doesn't know."

What is love?

Answer: It is not nearly as empty as the neighborhood is now, as the freshly re-shingled roof across the street, the black attic window beneath, or the night-hawk whistling its hunting song above. Not nearly as empty as the church steeple in its glaring night-gown of spotlight, or the wind-chimes on the porch next door, playing a song never heard before nor ever again. It is only as empty as the inevitable definition every life comes to, in this regard.

Four soldiers are brought before the leader of the opposing force.

"Welcome," says the general. "If you are cooperative, you will be treated properly. If you are not cooperative, you will be treated very improperly."

"We beg your pardon sir," says Soldier One, "but we believe there has been a mistake. We are actors. We were going to play your enemies in a brand new theatrical production in which your enemies lose the war."

"Is that so," says the general. "Where's the rest of your troupe?"

"They ran away," says One.

"Yes," says Two, "I agree. Very far away."

"What do they look like?"

"Just like your soldiers," says Two.

"And what is the name of your production," asks the general, and, while Soldiers One and Two are madly trying to remember, a young barmaid appears with a flagon of wine on a tray.

Soldier Three shouts, "Ana!" And the barmaid looks up in disbelief.

One elbows Three. "Yes, that's right," he says. "It's called Ana."

"Ana," the general says thoughtfully. He takes a long draft from the flagon and wipes his mouth with the back of his hand. "Strange name for a war play," he says.

"Well," says Two, "we were playing four soldiers from the losing side who return to a town captured by your army, in order to kidnap one of our girlfriends." One elbows Two.

"And her name is Ana."

"Is it a tragedy or a comedy?"

"A slapstick comedy," says One, and he slaps Two across the back of the head. The general laughs.

"No, it's Realism," says Two, and he starts strangling One. The general continues laughing, despite the change of genre.

"Tragedy," shouts Three, and he puts Two in a headlock, and all three stagger across stage in one another's arms. The general grabs his belly as a new wave of laughter crashes over him. Ana hits One and Two over the heads with her tray and runs away with Three. One and Two follow immediately, while the general dances and fires his pistol into the air, howling with glee. A tuba, a trumpet, and a gallon of moonshine are produced from the audience, and a Balkan party ensues.

Being in love is like...

Nicolae Ceausescu: Having all the blood in your body slowly replaced with another's, through the ethereal hum of a transfusion machine.

Elena Ceausescu: Opening the eyelids of a dead child and looking inside.

Three witches stand around a cauldron in a fog-shrouded vale.

"Do you see them in the cauldron's hideous broth," says Witch Two.

"No," says Three. "I told you already, I don't believe in this witchcraft bullshit, or any other superstitious religious mumbo jumbo."

"I see them," says One. "Our little spy has finally made contact and cleverly worked her way into their confidence, through one's inflamed passion. She now leads them to the execution of our desires."

"My sources verified that yesterday," says Three.

"Good. Good," says Two. "And they think they're making their own decisions?"

"Their desires make their decisions for them," says One.

"And we only think we control them because we understand their desires," says Three.

"So is it possible that we are controlled by their desires," asks Two.

"I thought I was playing the cynic here," says Three.

"Wait," says One, "I see the answer in the cauldron. Yes, it is possible that we are controlled by their desires."

"But we manipulate their desires," says Three.

"You mean our desires manipulate their desires," says Two.

"I suppose," says Three. "Then who are we that possess these desires?"

"The answer," says One, "it comes to me. Ah yes, only those who understand the limits of their freedom know they are free. Those who are free of all responsibility are no longer part of the world. They are ghosts."

"That didn't quite make sense," says Two.

"I think she means that freedom is defined by restraints," says Three. "Without any restraints, freedom loses all definition. For example, if you break your chains they are no longer chains. They become memories or symbols of chains. But if you forget about them completely they will manifest themselves as physical realities again."

"No," says One, "that's not exactly what I meant, though it sounds nice. I meant that those three horny soldiers only think they're free because they're horny."

"Now you lost me," says Three.

"Yes," says Two, "and we sent them some tail."

"But she's not sleeping with any of them, is she," says Three. "I hope not. Did you say 'tail'?"

"According to the cauldron she isn't," says One. "And this is exactly why they think they're free, because they're not doing what they feel they're expected to do."

"Oh, I see," says Two, "so we're free because we're making them do what we desire."

"Because then we're not doing it," says Three.

"The cauldron says yes," says One.

"Why don't you answer us yourself for once," says Three.

"Me? asks Two.

"No. Not you," says Three. She points at One. "You! Oh, look, the cauldron wants to know why you're always running the show."

"Listen, I don't need to be here," says One. "I can stop being a witch whenever I want. I can turn my back on our fog-shrouded haunts whenever I want. There, how was that for an answer?"

"That hurt my feelings," says Two.

"Yeah," says Three, "you didn't need to go that far."

How many communists does it take to fuck up a light bulb?

Answer: When he's young, Nicu's governesses won't let him play. He can't even play dead. It's not something you play at, they say. What you think you might love and what you think might love you are not the same thing.

Lover One: I'm chasing you because you're running.

Lover Two: I'm running because you're chasing.

Lover One: The faster you run the faster I'll chase.

Lover Two: You'll never get me.

Lover One: You'll never get away.

Lover Two: Touché.

Lover One: Touché.

What is loneliness?

Nicu falls in love with a woman. He loves her so much he wants to be with her always, including before they met. He wants to have her memories implanted into his own mind. To almost be her. But as she tells him the stories that he begs to hear, he begins to feel uneasy. She has done things he wouldn't have imagined she would have done. The farther they go into her past, the more she turns into someone else. These things bother him, and, because he loves her, they bother him even more. "I love her, so I must not let the incident with the wine bottle get to me," he tells himself. But it does. Precisely because he loves her. He too wants to be thrown from a rolling car, under exactly the same conditions, that he might break his own arm, that he might then understand, but he can't devise a plan that will satisfy such a desire without actually requiring him to live her entire life over again in her place. Finally, out of desperation, he decides that her past doesn't matter to him. What drew him in now pushes him away. "All that matters is that she's here, with me now," he thinks. "I don't care about who she was before I met her." And he is so sick of thinking about the wine bottle and the backstage pass and the rehab that he actually doesn't give a shit any more. And one day, voilá, it's gone. And one day, voilá, she's gone. And he hasn't murdered anyone. He just isn't in love any more. Or is he.

Answer: Is he.

Lover Two: I'm sorry. I can't love you because you want too much from me.

Lover One: I want too much from you because I'm afraid I will have nothing from you.

Lover Two: And you will have nothing.

Lover One: And you will too.

All sing together: Goodbye, goodbye, goodbye, goodbye, goodbye!

Nicu is in the castle's kitchen, late at night, making a sandwich after his first date.

The birds will not begin to sing for another hour or two. His unconceived brother enters and asks how it went.

His brother asks, "How far did you get?" Despite not existing, he is like many other brothers.

"Home," Nicu says.

"I can see that," says his brother, "but how about the date?"

"We went all the way."

"All the way to where," his brother says, looking around.

"I got to home base. We fucked."

"Home base," his brother says. "But you start at home base, don't you? Does that mean you fucked her before you fucked her?"

"Never mind," says Nicu. "You couldn't understand. You died before you even lived."

"But where are you when you're at home?"

Nicu shrugs.

"Who's home?"

"You're home, okay," Nicu says. "Are you happy now?"

Why did Nicolae Ceausescu fill his bathtub with milk?

Answer: In a time of famine, Nicolae fills his bathtub with cold milk and crawls in. When he's numb from the cold he begins to masturbate. He can't see his hand or genitalia through the milk, and it feels far away. It feels like someone else is doing it, perhaps in

Germany, or maybe Israel. He comes repeatedly, and then he slides under the surface and drinks of the milk until he vomits. Then he crawls out and orders the price of exit visas for Jews and Germans raised. "For failing," he mumbles as he signs the paperwork.

What is murder?

Answer: Two people cannot be one. Only if one dies can you stand before the window where the other one stood and take the crumpled suicide note in hand and read. Shut the window and turn to the ceaseless dark of the room and write it again and again till murder take it from you.

At evening we find the girl and the four soldiers passing a country church. The sky begins to boil and opens on them. They make a run for the shelter of the church, but just as they reach the doorway a skinny sweaty sexton blocks their path.

"Halt," says he. "Before you enter you must first answer a riddle."

"Are you mad," says Soldier One. "We're armed."

"Not anymore," says the sexton, and, to their amazement, they find their weapons are gone.

"They're inside," he says. "Well, except for this one." He raises Soldier Two's rifle in the air and squeezes off a round.

"How did you do that," says Two, looking down at his own hands.

"God did it. So, are you ready for my riddle?"

"Okay, hit us," says One.

"How do you know when you've been away too long?"

"How do you know when you've been away too long," repeats Soldier Three.

"Yes. Or how do you know when you've been alone too long? They're pretty much the same."

The five of them stand in the rain thinking.

"Don't answer too quickly," he says. "You only get one chance."

They stand in the rain a bit longer. Then Soldier Three has an idea. The others gather around while he tells them. No one has a better idea, so he turns to the Sexton.

"You know you've been alone too long when the sound of a zipper makes your mouth water," says Three.

"What?" He frowns at them. "That's possibly the stupidest answer I've ever heard."

"Is it the right answer," asks Two.

"No, you idiot."

A bolt of lightening strikes the dead elm in the cemetery across the road, and the sexton pauses and stares into the middle distance for a while. Our travelers stand in the rain, watching him stare at the burning tree.

"But it's close enough," he finally says. "Get inside."

———————

Nicu finds Rana sitting on a wall.

"Why do you place yourself in danger, when you can simply sit on the ground," asks Nicu.

"The ethical way to live must also be the religious way to live," says Rana. "Any day may kill me. The smallest thing such as sitting may kill me. And even smaller things may kill you, my boy. Blood is fickle. It loves you when it's with you, but it kills you the second it leaves. You must believe that it matters where you sit or what you eat."

"Okay," says Nicu. "But can't I simply do things because they seem logical or effective? Must they be holy?"

"The greatest reason is always the best reason. He who eats because he knows he will otherwise die understands the world better than he who eats because he is hungry."

"But if your body knows you're hungry, then why do you need to know?"

"Because, you incorrigible fool, as I've been saying over and over, your mind is nothing more than your body thinking!" Rana stands.

"But," Nicu says, "my instincts will keep me from death, out of an instinctive understanding of the world, and isn't an instinctive understanding the most complete understanding?"

"Why do you not want to die," asks Rana. "Dying is the most efficient way to preserve resources and avoid work. You see, your body is neither logical nor effective! Your body is an instinctive idiot! All decisions must be religious at the root!"

"But," Nicu begins to say.

"No more buts!" Rana grabs a loose stone from the top of the wall and throws it at Nicu with such force that he falls backwards off the wall.

The sexton tells them not to let the door hit their ass on the way out, and he ascends to his chamber. They draw close to one another on the cold stone floor and sleep.

Soldier One's dream:

He's an invisible presence in someone else's life. The other is a man, well-dressed, professional, perhaps an accountant or a financier. Now the man is in a bathroom. He stands with his hands submerged in a sink full of cold water. He's weeping in a most unprofessional manner. At least he's alone. At last. He's trying to get his wedding band off. It's burning. Out the window the river slivers through the black valley and a bright arterial transverse of traffic feeds the distant hills.

———————————

Soldier Two's dream:

He's a freelance bodyguard, and a man hires him because the man has been receiving threatening phone calls. After he's been working for the man a while, Two begins to suspect that the man's not entirely sane. For example, Two witnesses the man answering the phone when it hasn't rung. He begins to think perhaps the man is imagining the phone calls from which he's been hired to protect the man. Hence, Two's dilemma. Does he call a doctor? And what would that entail? Is the man, in fact, endangering his own life? And if so, how much force is permissible in order to protect the man from himself? For example, would a court of law acquit him if he were to hog tie the man for the man's own good? Should he quit his job? He's tempted to give the man a call, to give the man a reason to pay him. Then a voice thunders from the heavens, and only Two hears it. "What if you are both the same person," it says. "Don't be so quick to judge!"

———————————

Soldier Three's dream within a dream:

After making love to her, he falls into a fitful slumber where uncertainties bedevil him. What if he returned from the war and found she had supported herself by prostitution in his absence? How could he have ever known that such decisions might have to be made in a life? What other decisions might she have made? His eyes snap open and she's back beside him, breathing slowly. He sighs. She had not even been born yet when the war began. She's a lonely, beautiful fruit of the empire. And Three, like his father, is a farmer of its inland soil. For several years he dreamt he was murdering people on another planet, and then he was back. Back home. But something has changed. He rises and goes for a walk in the pasture. Beneath a shade tree he finds delicate, poisonous flowers. He tries to stomp them out. But they rise again from his footprints and spread like slender flames. He tries to keep his children away. But the flowers are picked and placed in a vase in the center of the feast laid out on the dining table, and the family eats to surfeit. And then they are hungry again. And the whole world is at the door, begging for a place at the table.

The Girl's dream:

She grows quickly in the vacuum outside her parents' suffocating love for one another. She's afraid of nothing but speaking. She runs across teetering railroad bridges, and she falls asleep reading *American Psycho* on the back of a grazing horse in the blazing midday sun. She meets the man who will ask her to marry him while she is volunteering in a war torn country. When she receives the news of her parents' fate she isn't shaken. She returns and accepts a position as one of the government's most feared functionaries. All this and she is still unable to speak without first bracing herself for the judgment she feels will certainly befall her. She is the last of their line.

Soldier Four's dream:

He is "I," and sometimes he imagines he's living in America in the Twenty-First Century. What an imagination, a woman says to him, as they eat breakfast together in the kitchen of a home on the edge of a freshwater sea. Is it possible, she says, to know who one is from within a dream? Is it even possible to understand one's life from within one's life?

Answer: Is it possible not to?

———————————

Taking a shortcut through a Bucharest alley in the dead of night, Nicu trips over his biological father. Nicu Senior lies in a puddle of his own urine, head propped against a warehouse, smoking a joint he's barely managed to roll. Neither of them know who the other is. Nevertheless, Nicu Senior says, "It's about time." And he proceeds to tell Nicu Junior a joke.

This is the joke: A father falls asleep on the couch, with his infant son sleeping on his chest. It's a time of famine in his dream, and he's entered a forest to gather berries, nuts, pickles, and whatnot for his family. He hears grunting and snorting behind him, and, just as he turns, a wild boar charges from the undergrowth and knocks him to the ground. He locks his arms around the beast's neck and squeezes with all his might. It shakes him, squealing, and digs its tusks into his belly, but he won't let go. If he lets go he'll lose control. He sees his blood speckling the leaves, but he holds on until its body is still. Night's falling, and he realizes he's too far from home to return before dark, so he lies down in the leaves and hauls the body of the boar onto his chest, and, as its heat slowly passes into him, he hears a woman's voice through the trees. She's crying. No, she's screaming. But she doesn't sound angry. She sounds very sad. Yes, the man tells himself, she knows that I may never be back. Yes, the man tells himself, this is probably the best interpretation.

"So," Nicu Senior says, "what do you think?"

"What do you mean," says Nicu Junior.

"What do you think of my joke?"

"I think if you think that was a joke you need serious help," he says, and takes off running. His father screams something unintelligible after him, and this is the first and the last time they meet each other in life. Nicu Junior thinks Nicu Senior is merely a dissipated lunatic he met one night in an alley. Which, in a sense, is absolutely true.

———————

Nicu asks Rana what he thinks about genius. Rana says it doesn't exist, that only work and obsession exist.

"Love and genius are misnomers for degrees of obsession and work," he says. "No matter how smart people think you are, you'll only have one original idea in your life."

He looks at Nicu.

"And in your case," he says, "you'll probably be asleep."

———————

Being in love is like…

Nicu: The building up of memories into being.

Ana: A river dammed, by its own debris, into a body.

———————

Nicu decides not to be sad about the unfathomableness of life anymore. He sits under the willow and writes down everything he knows to be true, a prayer of sorts. When he has over a hundred certainties recorded, Rana appears on the path.

"What are you doing," he asks.

"I'm writing down everything that I know to be true."

"Why would you waste your time doing that?"

"So when I get depressed about how ignorant I am, I can look in my book and be assured that I know something."

While Nicu is still exhaling the word "something," Rana snatches the journal from his hands and throws it over the edge of the cliff.

"That's the most important thing to know about knowledge," Rana says. "Unless you have the power to banish fire from the world, you have to write things that can be burned."

Nicu is in shock. Rana slaps him across the face. "Wake up," he says.

Nicu wakes up and cries, "I hate you!"

"Much better. Now write that down," Rana says, and continues on his way.

————————————

His head hurts all day and makes his usual toil more toilsome than usual. A sharp pain in his temples and a throbbing behind his eyes and finally, when he gets home, he removes his glasses and grinds the heels of his palms into his eyes, and he begins to cry, and the crying turns to sobbing, and he can't tell how long it has been, but, when he stops it's dark out, and the pain has gone, and then, only then, does he realize that he hadn't cried because it had hurt. It had hurt because he had wanted so badly to cry.

Answer: Every man is a question he asks himself. He is every joke for which the punch line is death. He is every story for which there is a moral. Yet, the moral is not he.

————————————

Nicu lies on the straw cot in his stone cell, moaning. He has an ear infection that has gone untreated. He can no longer hear with his right ear, which is oozing yellow pus. He grimaces at the ceiling and imagines ways to puncture his eardrum to release the excruciating pressure. He rolls off the cot and kneels beside it and prays.

"Lord, please stop popping my cherry," he says.

There's knocking at the door of his cell.

He doesn't hear it.

The knocking grows louder.

"Who's there," he shouts.

"Stop your ears by pressing, and your rectum by contracting, and enter the sound of sound," says a voice.

He's not sure he heard correctly. "What did you say," he shouts.

He hears what sounds like slobbering on the other side of the door. "Put your blood to the door," it says. "Become the sucking. When you sneeze," it says, "be uninterruptedly aware."

"Who's there," Nicu shouts.

"Be the unsame same," it says. "Enter the sound of your name and through this sound all sounds."

"Who's there?"

"Open the door."

"Who are you?"

The Sexton's dream:

A woman and her husband drive from the Midwestern town where they had settled after the war to The Grand Canyon over Christmas vacation. Her husband badgers her into it. They haven't been getting along particularly well for a while now. He still loves her, but has taken to taking their relationship for granted. He's also a perfectionist and keeps complaining about this and that, and she thinks he's complaining about her. Well, she doesn't die by her own hand. This time she takes control. As her husband is peering over the rim of the canyon, in one of his rare moments of silence, she pushes him. He doesn't scream like she imagines he would. He falls very apologetically, and no one but her is witness to the fall.

At the wake, the world in the casket is hidden. It's closed, and she cries, "Why? Why?" The people around her think she's asking God why he killed her husband, but in reality she's asking herself why she killed her husband. You see, she simply isn't finishing the sentence, and others so love to finish our sentences for us that they protect us from ourselves. You see, she doesn't remember exactly why she did it. And to feel avenged she would have to remember exactly why. This is what she's asking God. It has turned to a hideous rot at the core of her being. "Why? she cries. She can't remember. "Why!" And for once she's alone to figure it out, without him giving his lousy two-cents-worth. No, he's not there. Only she, in her somewhat over-the-hill, yet radiant deathless beauty. Wouldn't that be nice.

One morning, Rana doesn't come to breakfast. Nicu eats alone in the great hall. After eating, he goes to Rana's quarters. He isn't there either. Nicu searches the whole monastery, asking everyone he meets if they've seen his master. Some can't answer due to vows of silence. Others answer but are less helpful than the silent. Finally, Nicu decides to proceed with his lessons on his own, as if Rana were there, but the day is now not only a drudgery, but a lonely drudgery as well. "I'll do whatever he wants tomorrow," Nicu tells himself, "and I won't complain, as long as he's there."

That night God comes to Nicu in a dream.
    "Lord," he begs, "tell me what to do."

"You were fucked into being," says God, "and you shall be fucked right out again."

"Thank you, Lord," Nicu says, "you are always right."

What does "American Dream" really mean?

Answer: Well, technically, it would have to mean any dream an American has. For example, right now an American is dreaming that he's a soldier marching to war with the Austro-Hungarian Empire. His platoon runs into a factory and gets on a service elevator. There isn't room for him and one of the other enlisted men, so they take the stairs and end up in the food court. They decide to have a bottle of wine and a couple grilled cheese sandwiches. He realizes his wife is probably worried about him, so he asks the other soldier if he can borrow his cell phone so he can tell his wife that he isn't missing in action. He's just having lunch. But as soon as the phone is handed over, it starts ringing, so the American answers it. It's Jacqueline Lee Bouvier Kennedy Onassis. She's locked in the women's restroom, and wants him to let her out. So he does. Then she gives him a blow job. The dream dialogue is conducted in approximately thirty-six different languages, but they all sound like Texan English. This is a good example of an "American Dream."

Nicolae Ceaucescu calls the future. When it answers he says, "Is this Edward?"

"Uh huh," it says.

"Our target has been located."

"Where?"

"Three five seven five Oakland Avenue, apartment one zero six, Milwaukee, Wisconsin."

"Got it."

"The payment will be in the usual place."

"Uh huh."

"It's been a pleasure, as usual."

"For today's lesson, you must repeat after me," says Rana. "What touches my flesh is touched by my flesh."

"What touches my flesh is touched by my flesh."

"Who does right by me is by me righted."

"Who does right by me is by me righted."

"The suffering servant serves knowledge best."

"The suffering servant serves knowledge best."

"The manager manages to manage his anger."

"The manager manages to manage his anger."

"His organs are organized in an organic order."

"His organs are organized in an organic order."

"The bludgeoned curmudgeon sits in the dungeon."

"The bludgeoned curmudgeon sits in the dungeon."

"I will say anything I am told to say."

"I will say anything I am told to say."

"I would like my master to touch me in a bad way."

"I would like my master to touch me in a bad way."

"Why you!" Rana starts beating Nicu with his cane.

After leaving the church, the four soldiers and the girl follow a footpath into the beech forests at the lower reaches of the mountain. Once inside the corridor of trees, Soldier Two produces a ceremonial urn from his sack. "Got us a little insurance policy here," says he, "courtesy of the sacristy."

"Is that real silver," says One.

"Of course. Look how tarnished it is."

"Give it to me." One grabs it and starts rubbing it with the sleeve of his coat. It starts smoking. "What the hell," he says, and drops it into the leaves.

The lid skitters away, and a cloud of milky smoke disgorges itself from the urn. It neither disperses nor rises, but swells into the shape and size of a woman who stands undulating from the mouth of the overturned vessel. With a sudden hiss, capillaries of scarlet light fill the form. It speaks, and its voice is like a crackling of flame.

"I am the suicide," it says. "I am the death that drove my lover mad. Now I live in fire. Wherever a candle burns I am there, looking into the darkness. Wherever there is a campfire there is a window through which I watch the wilderness, the fangs ringing the ring of light. Wherever a torch disappears down an ennitered corridor I too disappear. I am the razor thin division between what is known and what is not. Whatever is incinerated, ignited, cremated, whatever fuels your world, I go through, molecule by molecule. My world is a crimson window into yours, glowing and growing, until one day it shall be all that you too can see. Until all your world is on my side and a great shade is drawn against the permanent night. Every star in the firmament is a great eye…"

Three has quietly retrieved the lid from the side of the trail and clamped it back on the urn, severing the infernal figure from its source. It instantly turns into an ordinary cloud of sulfurous smoke, and drifts into the understory of the forest, where it confuses itself into nothing amongst the trunks of the trees.

Three hands the urn back to Two. "Here you go," he says.

"Keep a lid on that shit," says One.

And on they trudge.

———————————

Being in love is like…

Yoshio Iwasaki: Descending into a tank of formaldehyde with a toothbrush to scrub algae from comrade Lenin's nose.

Zoia: Being God's tongue.

———————————

"Imagine your personal space," says Rana.
"Done."
"Now, imagine it expanding."
"Actually," says Nicu, "I have to confess. I don't believe in personal space."
"You don't have to believe in it to imagine it."
"How can you imagine something you don't believe?"
"You can imagine Santa Claus, can't you?"
"I suppose."
"Now, what's the essence of Santa Claus?"
"Gluttony?"
"No. In your mind, what is it that allows the image of something you don't believe to appear?"
Nicu is silent.
"Okay, let me rephrase that. What makes Santa Claus tick?"
"What makes Santa Claus tick."
"Yes."
"His heart?"
"You idiot." Rana slaps Nicu across the face. "Get out of my sight!"
Nicu runs from the room sniveling.

———————————

What should you do if you find a Hungarian standing on a landmine? If he begs you to help him? If he says, "I was taking this shortcut to the next village, daydreaming about the girl who's waiting for me, when I felt a mechanical snap underfoot and instantly remembered that this valley was a green line during the war. I froze as soon as the thought struck me, and I've been standing here ever since.* Please help me. She'll think I forgot her."

Answer #1: If you're Nicu Senior, ask him for the girl's name, and when he tells you, assure him that you'll make sure she has a good time. Then tell him who you are. Walk in circles around him, giving him little shoves, telling him what you're going to do to his girl. Start walking in the direction of the village, and when you're far enough away to avoid injury to yourself, turn and throw several large rocks at him. Laugh hysterically as he attempts to dodge the missiles without moving. When you get into the woods, circle back to the edge of the tree line and watch him shake until it gets dark. He's your work of art now. You've outdone the man who planted the landmine. Now, where were you? Ah, yes, the girl.

*Editorial note: According to a landmine expert I had cocktails with in Beirut, there are no landmines that detonate upon release. Certain booby-traps will, but not landmines. Except, he pointed out, in certain Angelina Jolie movies. And, apparently, in certain joke books.

Rana takes Nicu to a mountaintop observation platform, gives him a pair of binoculars and points his attention into the mountain pass below.

"What do you see," he asks.

"A waterfall."

"To the right of that."

"Oh, I see. Five men. No, four men and a woman."

"What more can you see?"

"Uh, some trees."

"No, about the people."

"Oh, um, the woman is falling behind."

"Yes."

"She looks strong. They've probably had a disagreement. The men have deserted the army and are returning to their homes in different provinces. She was a lover or a, hey, I think she's looking at us."

"Don't be foolish. Now, look over here. He points to a distant mountain peak. What do you see?"

"Three witches standing around a bubbling cauldron."

"What? Give me those!" Rana snatches the binoculars from Nicu and applies them to the distance. "I can't believe it," he says. "I thought they were dead. Well, it looks like I've got my work cut out for me. Oh shit, they're looking this way. Shit! They see me! Now they know that I know that they're there! I've lost my advantage!"

He drops the binoculars and starts running. "Fuck me!" he yells.

———————

What should you do if you find a Hungarian standing on a landmine? If he's shivering and his eyes are red and swollen? If he smells strongly of sweat, urine, feces, and vomit and says, in a hoarse voice, "Oh thank god, I have to get to my girlfriend immediately. I've been standing here all night. A bear came and sniffed me and I think it would have eaten me if I hadn't thrown up on it. Please help me. You're soldiers. You can go back and get your landmine defusing thing, back at… back at… where did you come from?"

Answer #2: I can't believe I had to ask. He's just realized that you're deserters, but he doesn't know who you are, and he can't defend himself or tell the authorities. In fact, he and all his testimony could soon be gone forever, and it wouldn't be your fault. Also, he was going to see his girlfriend, so he probably has money on him. Ah, beautiful Reason! Thank god you're human! What are you waiting for? Rob him. Then you can try to put him off balance when you get far enough away, to avoid the possibility of him telling the next passerby. But how far is far enough? Oh hell, you're civilized, and he seems to be doing himself in just fine. Just get the money. And the jacket. But make sure he takes it off very carefully.

Witch One: "That witless apprentice of his has blown our cover."

"What do we do now?"

"I'm not sure."

"Me neither. I don't trust my free will anymore."

"Let's let the reader decide."

"Oh, you wicked girl! What a delicious idea."

"Where is it?"

"Over here."

"I see. Alright, dear reader, here are the choices. Either the old fart hunts us down, one by one, and dispatches each of us in some psychosexual, sadomasochistic fashion, or one of us goes over there and teaches the old goat a lesson he'll not likely forget."

"Kick his ever-living ass."

"Yeah."

"Don't worry, dear reader. No matter what choice you think you've made, we will know what your true choice is. The deepest desires of your unconscious are but a children's book to us. With us you cannot make a wrong choice. Now, think it over carefully. Get a feel for it. Sleep on it."

"Yeah."

As they pass through the mountains, the four soldiers and the girl encounter an old man working on a bridge that spans a narrow chasm into which disappears a waterfall. The soldiers are apprehensive to approach. They draw close to confer by the side of the trail.

"What if he recognizes that we're deserters," says Three.

"You weren't concerned when you dragged us back to the city, or when we sought shelter in the church," says Two.

"We're getting closer to home," says Three.

"He's got a point," says One.

"But this is the only pass for thirty miles," says Two.

They all look at Four. He says nothing.

The girl is not consulted.

"Looks like we'll have to throw him off the cliff," says One.

No one says anything. They start walking again.

When they approach, the old man looks up. "Goodness," he says, "you startled me. What timing you have. I think I might finish the bridge today."

"Are you working on it alone," One asks.

"Oh yes," says the old man. "I've been working on it alone for six years now, translating trees into struts and planks and pegs and pillars. There's my hut over there. And there's my goat."

"Who on earth could wait this long for a bridge to be built," says Three.

"Oh," the old man says, "I'm not working for anyone."

"Well," says Three, "then why on earth are you doing this?"

"Because six years ago, when I was away, selling charcoal in the city, my wife was murdered by a thief who broke into our home. The thief was caught, and the townsfolk gave me the choice of what to do with him. I couldn't think. I wanted him dead. I wanted him alive so he could suffer. I wanted him to know who he'd killed. I wanted my wife back. I told them to hold onto him. I said, 'I'm going away for a while to think about it.' And here I came."

"Why did you come here," says Two.

"Because this is the most dangerous trail through the mountains." He points at the waterfall. "Until now, travelers have had to cross the slippery rocks behind the water, and every year someone slips into the abyss. I came here and sat on the ground where you now stand, and I thought about my wife and I thought about that man, and about killing him, and I said to myself, 'I'm going to build a bridge for my wife.'"

"And what about the thief," says Two.

"They're still waiting for my decision."

"And what's your decision," says One.

The old man looks at his bridge and sighs. "I suppose when I'm done I'll go back down there and I'll tell them to let him go. But not until I'm done."

"But that's today," says Two.

"Oh, perhaps. Perhaps it will take a bit longer. It's safe to cross now, in fact. I'm just fine-tuning it." He stares into the valley and says, "I loved my wife very much." He goes on staring like that for a while. The rest of them look at Soldier One, who, feeling their eyes on him, shrugs.

"Well, old man," he says, "good luck."

"Good luck," they all say, and all but the girl begin crossing the bridge. She lingers beside the old man who is still staring into the valley.

———————

"That's it," says One. "The reader has decided already."

"Which of us should go then?"

"I will," says Three.

"Thank god," says Two. "We'll miss you, Zoia."

"No you won't. The moment I leave, I will cease to have ever been as I now am."

"I think what Ana means," says One, "is that we miss you now, in anticipation of having never known you. And now is forever."

"Yeah."
"Thanks, guys. I miss you too."

———————

The girl touches the old man's shoulder and, unnoticed by all, disappears behind the veil of the waterfall.

The old man returns to work.

———————

Nicolae Ceaucescu calls the future again.

"You're fired," he screams. "Absofuckinglutely fired!"

He stands silent for a moment, listening to the future, mouth hanging open as if he's watching a giant beaver take a shit on a grand piano.

"What's not to understand," he says. "You're fired!"

———————

What is love?

Soldier Four:

———————

Out of the changing maples emerges the girl, naked, wet, and trembling as a newborn, a motley of edelweiss, saxifrage, yellow poppy, and transylvanian columbine petals clinging to her. She advances upon the iron gates of the monastery.

"Females aren't allowed within the sacred enclosure," a skinny sweaty monk says to her through the bars.

"I'm here for Rana," she says. "If you don't want me coming inside, send him out."

"Neither may a woman's words enter the enclosure."

"You seem to be hearing me just fine. Tell him Zoia's here."

The monk squints at her and says, "I can't hear you."

"Have it your way," she says, and throws the gates open, knocking the monk on his skinny sweaty ass. She enters.

"How'd you do that," the monk whines.

"It wasn't locked, you idiot. Now," she raises her voice and sets the very air ringing. "Rana! Where are you?"

A crowd of monks gathers around her. "Be gone, female," they hiss, "Go hence amongst the bitches and heifers and fuck thyself! Be gone from this hallowed earth! Less thy very shadow defile it!"

"Grow up," she says.

Rana emerges from the temple, says, "What the fuck's going on," and descends the steps in the direction of the commotion. Nicu stays at the top of the steps and watches, arms folded into the sleeves of his robe.

The monks part, allowing Rana to stand before the young woman. "Well well well," says Rana, "Look who we have here. Couldn't wait for me, could you. You know what we do to women around here, don't you?"

"Same thing you do to them everywhere?"

"That's right." And with that he unties the sash of his robe and throws it wide, exposing an enormous, erect phallus.

The girl gives it a swift kick, jamming it into his abdominal cavity, leaving nothing but a tiny nub protruding like the head of a newly hatched chick from a nest of louse-infested hair. Rana sinks to his knees and bows his head for a minute. A murmur passes through the crowd. He carefully re-covers his nakedness and ties the sash. He then stands and smiles, revealing vampiric canines. "If you want it that way," he says.

He encircles the girl with his arms and thrusts his fangs at her neck.

She turns into a pine tree, against which he smashes his face.

"You fuffing bish," he howls, staggering backwards. He stands for another minute, thinking and wiping pink foam from his lips. Then he turns into a giant prehistoric beaver with incisors the size of fists, and he falls onto the tree again.

The air is filled with a tinkling, creaking sound, like a time-lapse recording of a lake freezing, and the beaver looses a pitiful moan and falls onto its back. It lies there, spread eagle, its naked prehistoric belly exposed. A monk steps forward and knocks on the tree. "It's petrified wood," he says. Then he raises from the ground, one in each hand, a pair of giant incisors. The crowd goes, "Ohhhh…" They turn their gaze back to the beaver, which is now a man again, face bloodied and mumbling. He rolls over onto his hands and knees and screams.

The scream turns to a roar, and a brontosaurus stands over them now, a leg in each corner of the courtyard, tail brushing the cornice of the temple. When its lungs are empty, the beast raises its right foreleg and brings it down on the pine tree with such might that the buildings rattle on their foundations and at least one more monk is knocked on his ass.

Then there's silence. Silence and no sign of a tree under the creature's foot. Only the stock-still silence of the beast, whose eyes are wider than it was ever possible for a brontosaurus's eyes to be. It shudders the full length of its frame and empties its lungs in a gust so powerful it empties the apple tree of its bounty, and the beast tumbles over, flattening the garden and a thirty foot stretch of the monastery's outer wall. Only then do they notice that its right foreleg has mushroomed outward at the foot, where it exploded over the giant diamond now snuggled serenely in a three-foot crater in the courtyard cobblestones.

Rana limps out of the garden. "I've got you now," he mumbles. And disappears.

The congregation gasps in unison.

Just then the monastery's financial manager runs from his cell screaming, waving a copy of the *Wall Street Journal* over his head.

"The diamond market is plummeting, he screams, diamonds are worthless! We're ruined!"

He stops and thinks. "No! Wait! Now's the time to buy! Buy!" He runs back to his cell screaming, "Buy!"

The rest of the monks grin and fix their gaze on the giant diamond before them.

"The market is trembling," the manager screams from his cell. "It's shaking! It's groaning! It's sweating like mad! Oh fuck! It just bottomed out! I think we really are fucked this time!"

Rana collapses into an insensate heap beside the diamond.

The diamond turns back into the girl. She sits on the edge of her little crater, elbows on knees, panting for breath. Rana regains consciousness long enough to say, "You win, bitch," and passes out again.

Nicu rushes to the side of the girl. He helps her to her feet.

"Traitor," Rana moans, and passes out again.

"Who are you," Nicu says.

"Zoia," she says.

"Why are you here," he says.

"To do what I just did," she says. "Why are you here?"

"I'm watching the world for God," he says.

"I'm getting dizzy," she says.

"Come with me," he says, and leads her to the stable at the edge of the courtyard.

———————

A young man climbs a mountain so he can speak to the old man at the summit.

"What's your question," says the old man.

"I'm a bit embarrassed to ask," says the young man.

"You just climbed a mountain," says the old man. "Now isn't the time to be bashful. Spit it out."

"Well, I just wanted to know where you shit."

"Ah, a smart ass," says the old man. "Well, I'll give you a hint. There wasn't a mountain here when I first sat down."

"That's what I feared," says the young man.

"Well, now that you know the secret," says the old man, "beat it! Go make yourself a mountain and leave me alone. Wise ass."

After kicking Rana's ass, Zoia is allowed to convalesce in the hay mow above the sheep stable. After having his ass kicked, Rana locks himself in his cell. Nicu spends every moment of the following days with the girl above the stable, either tending her nominal wounds or utterly consumed with her in the passion of conversational, oral, manual, vaginal, anal, and cleftual intercourse. The monks who happen to repeatedly overhear the lovemaking clap their hands over their ears, contort their faces in silent heavenward cries of anguish, run from the stable to their cells, beat their rebellious members into submission, and pray for Rana's speedy recovery and speedier revenge. One pious monk documents the trials of his spirit in a tract entitled, "When Thunder Poundeth at the Heads of God's Sheep."

When Rana does finally emerge from his cell a week later, he looks as bad as when he entered it, but he has a travel bag slung over his shoulder. The monks surround him, begging for justice. He tells them to fuck off, then crosses the courtyard in the direction of the stable. Zoia emerges and stands in his path.

"Fuck you, bitch," he says, "I'm not interested in you. Where's the boy?"

Nicu emerges from the stable, brushing straw from his robe. "Yes, master?"

"Congratulations. You're done with your training. I have to go now."

"What?"

"I said you're done," he says.

"But we just started."

"No." He sighs. "You've successfully completed the entire course. Now, if you don't mind, I've got witches to hunt." He turns and begins walking toward the road.

Nicu stands with his mouth agape.

Rana pauses at the edge of the road and turns around. "Oh for Chrissakes, okay, you have one last lesson to learn."

"What is it?"

"Well, you have a choice. The last lesson is a choice. Either I explain the seven stages of existence, the fourth of which begins after the expiration of the four-dimensional manifestation of your being, or I unveil for you the mystery of transmigration, by turning you into an asshole."

"Is that supposed to be a joke?"

However you want to interpret it.

"Okay, turn me into an asshole."

"Done."

Rana, as a young man, loves a girl who will kill herself, and she loves him with equal passion. They always save the last bite of food for the other. They find, or make, small gifts for each other, each day, because they know how living on earth can be. Tonight, for example, as they eat canned beans and stale bread, Rana tickles Ana's knees under the table with an owl feather he found on the way to work at the mirror factory. Ana giggles and accepts the gift. Then she slides a small box across the table. Inside is a champagne cork. Rana makes a popping sound with his lips and throws the cork in the air. Ana laughs. From his fist he pours her, and then himself, an invisible glass of champagne. They raise their glasses and he says, "To comrade Ceausescu's health!" Ana laughs again, and they drink. This is one of many nights. But the future is full of nights without her.

What should you do if you find a Hungarian standing on a landmine? If he's actually sitting on the landmine now, with his arms around his knees, rocking back and forth? If, when he sees you, he stops and says quietly, "I've gone mad. Ana, is that you? How could it be? Did he find you? Did he tell you?" If he carefully rises, using his hand to transfer his body weight from his buttocks to his foot? "What did he do to you?"

Answer: Say, "My name is Zoia. I'm here to help you. Cheer up. You and I have the whole world ahead of us now." Give him a drink from your canteen. Have a drink yourself. Now, to work. Pile soil up beneath him, around the earthbound leg, all the way up to his crotch, so it looks like he's stepped into a foxhole. Pack the dirt down as hard as you can, leaving it loose enough just around the leg so he can rapidly withdraw it as he falls backward down the little hill you have built under him. Now kiss him long and hard, in case it doesn't work, and shove him away from you as hard as you possibly can.

At the end, Nicolae and Elena Ceausescu won't be captured and shot to death by a zealous band of soldiers in a small, dingy courtyard somewhere on television. The murderous tyrants will walk across the border, across Ukraine, disguised as begging gypsies, to the pastoral paradise of my parents' Poland, to an airport that will take them to America. They will walk into a new life where their old life will warm them like a distant bonfire seen through flowering linden trees. They will walk and walk, through the temporality of their own cruelty, to a small farm with a small garden with the smallest, sweetest cabbages in all of Wisconsin. They will both be happy. Elena will sing Romanian folksongs while cleaning the little cabin. Nicolae will chuckle softly in the garden.

"What are you laughing at, Nicolae," Elena will ask.

"Nothing, my dove," he will say, "nothing at all."

Four soldiers say goodbye to one another at the intersection of two roads. Two continue on the path they'd all been following. The other two go in opposite directions down the transverse path. They all walk for two days more, stopping only to curl up in the tall grass at the side of the road to sleep.

At the end of the second day, they each arrive at a thatched clay-brick hut, at the door of which is a crying hag. Each soldier runs to her and engulfs her in his arms and says, "Mother, mother, I've missed you so."

After a moment, he looks around and says, "Where are my father and my brothers and sisters?"

And she says, "They've all gone looking for you. Until I saw you on the road I thought none of you would return, and now I think only you will."

"Well," says the soldier, "if we keep thinking that, then we'll be content with each other, and if they do return, we'll feel we've been given a gift."

And they enter the hut, and all over the country lonely streamers of smoke unfurl from the chimneys.

Rana sits in the corner of an empty, dimly lit saloon. His head is bowed, in meditation it seems. The floorboards wheeze beneath your feet, dear reader, and he looks up.

"Trying to sneak up on me, eh," he says. "Grown weary of the jokes have we? You'd like me to finally get down to business. Explain to you why you're here. Perhaps you've prepared yourself for my cruelty. Or maybe you approach out of a sincere desire to learn. Perhaps your desire is so great you're willing to leave yourself forever. This must be the case, or I must simply beat you as I do Nicu. I must beat you within an inch of your life. Every moment of your life. This, finally, is no joke. Enlightenment is the worst thing that can befall a man. Enlightenment or my fist. Return to your jokes, I say. Turn back. Leave the education to him. Yes, that's it. Turn. I'm the true sphinx, for you'll never solve my riddle. The second you think you have the answer, the question will have changed. That's it. Turn."

AMERICAN FABLES

Beaver has been recently touched, gently but firmly.
He sees god everywhere now.
Here it is, this very minute, in his feces.

God speaks to him, but he can't understand it.
It sounds like shit.
"There's a catfish on the moon," it seems to say.

This Catfish has a fish bowl over her head.
She stands at the peak of Mons Pico, staring at the vast shadow
it casts onto the Mare Imbrium basin.
Catfish has her thumb in the air, as if to check perspective, or
maybe hitch a ride.

Muskrat only wanted to have sex with Catfish as often and in
as many ways as inhumanly possible.
Catfish only wanted to get involved with someone, or, in other
words, to inextricably intertwine her fate with that of another.
They did.

Now there's a special place in Muskrat's heart for hell.
A tiny room, identical to heaven in every regard, with the
exception that, of course, it's not heaven.
It's renowned throughout all of hell as the most perverse of
punishments.

Inside the room is a universe.
Inside the universe is a moon.
Standing atop one of the tallest mountains of that moon is Catfish, trying not to think about Muskrat.

Beaver stares at his poop, trying to figure out what it's trying to say, wondering if maybe he should bury it.
Catfish stares at her mountainous shadow.
She's thinking about god now, wondering if it got her message and, if so, what it's going to do about it.

What they both see resembles a black pyramid.
From its tip a white speck grows slowly larger.
It becomes a small craft, on what they now see is a long, dark, unbending runway, stretching from the horizon before them to the horizon behind.

The craft stops, and the passenger window rolls down.
Beaver is at the wheel.
"If you can read a map," he says, "get in."

Setting eyes on a fetching young muskrat is the most dangerous thing a female can do.
More than drinking with strangers or walking alone at night.
She might do whatever he asks, and he might ask for something he doesn't know he doesn't want.

He might ask if he can have sex with your feet.
Then he might beg you to please never tell anyone about it.
Then he might start looking at your feet strangely, and he might ask you to please cover them from now on.

Or he might never tire of your feet.
Though your heart may resent the blood it must send there.
And long for the days when your self was indivisible.

The past grows smaller as you move.

The unseen enters view.

Tiny trees and houses and cars below you.

You see Muskrat in one of the cars.

He's driving to his sister-in-law's cabin up north.

He's thinking the worst thing that can happen to a muskrat is to fall in love with a catfish that loves you, because, as soon as she knows you're in love with her, she'll do anything you ask, whether she really wants it or not, and how can you be expected to make all the right decisions for two people, when you can hardly make a single right decision for yourself.

"What's on your mind," Beaver asks.

"What's the name of this ship," Catfish asks.

"*Muskrat*," he says.

"What a coincidence," Catfish mumbles.

"What did you say?"

"Nothing."

Muskrat flies out past the last street light in town, into the wilderness of space, into the heart of the system.

Catfish's niece, Catbird, answers the door.

She looks exactly like Catfish, but younger, and a bird.

"Is your aunt here," he asks.

"No one's here except me," she says. "I come here to get away from everyone."

"Sorry," he says, "I've looked everywhere but here, so I thought maybe this would be the magic door."

"It's okay," she says. "You look tired. Would you like to come in?"

Over a cup of coffee, Catbird asks, "Do you know why she left you?"

"I think she thinks I don't love her," he says. "I think she thinks I think she's a sexual object."

"You've come a long way for a sexual object," Catbird says.

Muskrat raises an eyebrow and says, "You think I'm a sexual object?"

Catbird smiles and says, "I don't objectify people like that, unless they've got a hot ass."

"Okay, I admit it," he says. "I think she's a smart, complex, and, consequently, often irritating, sexual object I think I love."

"Often irritating," Catbird repeats.

"Yes, there's that," Muskrat says, "but I don't think that makes me inconsistent."

"No," Catbird says, "It proves that you're complex too."

"A complex object."

"Perhaps she's with someone else now," she says.

"I don't think so," he says.

"If she's anything like my mother," she says.

He frowns.

"People say I look a lot like her," Catbird says. "Do you think so?"

"Yes," he says.

"Except I don't have anyone who would drive up here looking for me," she says. "Never have."

"You're lying," he says.

"I don't lie," she says. "That's why I'm up here, trying to figure out what's wrong with me."

"What you're feeling is perfectly normal for the young and inexperienced," he says. "You just need time and, well, experience."

"You're assuming I'm inexperienced," she says.

"Well, either that or young," he says.

"Well, I'm both," she says, "and I'd rather not be."

"I feel awkward around objects," she says. "I usually insult them, unintentionally. I would like someone I trust to teach me how to lie."

"I don't know how to lie," he says.

"And yet you just did," she says.

"You think a lot like her too," he says.

"I trust you," she says. "And I'm very discreet. I would never do anything to hurt my aunt, whom we both love so very much."

Muskrat flies past the asteroid belt and the burning planets, and banks, on the gravitational well of the sun, into nothing.

On the other side of nothing, *Muskrat* hangs frozen over a colorful fair that expands to a vanishing point in every direction.

The air glows as if light itself.

"Welcome to the Market Between Worlds," says Beaver.

"Should we land," asks Catfish.

"No," says Beaver, "If the ship moves a micron, it will be catapulted back into our dimension at light speed, but you and I are immaterial, so we can hop down there and look around."

Muskrat has gone so far into nothingness it has become somethingness.

Emptiness becomes space becomes distance becomes dimension becomes form becomes object becomes sexual.

Intercourse becomes exchange as far as the eye can see.

"It becomes you," says Beaver.

Catfish is trying on new fishbowls at one of endless stands.

The fair swarms around them, a panoply of pure beings being every world in representation.

Catfish removes the last fish bowl.

She sets it on the display table, beside her own, and looks at them and sighs.

She turns away from them.

"You look sad," says Beaver.

"I have no idea what I'm looking for," she says.

"Well then, we need to find you an idea."

At the first idea booth they approach, Locust whispers to them, "Silence is the key to happiness, to achieve complete silence in all things, in thought, expression, and spirit," and then he was silent.

"How do you do that," asks Catfish.

Locust points to a sign above his head that reads, "For details, give me the rest of your life."

Every booth is the same.

They tantalize Catfish with their beliefs but demand her life in exchange for explanations.

"The key to happiness is sex," says Mule, "lots and lots of sex."

"Each of us is a totality unto our self, the beginning and the end and the center of all creation," says Hyena.

"Each of us is a different incarnation of the same god," says Platypus.

"We are all utterly alone, in an alien world, and can only touch one another with violence," says Penguin.

"What we call life is the conversion of time into experience," says Slime Mold, "and death the return of experience to time."

"Trying to understand the meaning of life is like trying to hide a watermelon quickly," says Mongoose. "I wouldn't recommend it."

"I can tell your future by reading the stains in your underwear," says Weasel.

"No thanks," says Catfish.

"If you're shy, I can turn around while you take them off."

"No thanks, really."

"The key to happiness is learning to love pain and loneliness," says Lemming.

"When we fall asleep, when we fall into the blackness beneath dream, we are all in the same place, the one pure consciousness that is all consciousness," says Jumping Mouse.

"As soon as someone figures out what god is trying to say, the world will end," says Termite.

"The universe is run by venereal diseases that every day fight great dynastic wars of ascendancy," says Maggot.

"The point," says Tiger, "is to love existence to the point that existence ceases to exist."

"The meaning of life is known only to the mad," says Tortoise.

"At least once in your life be the first to a party and the last to leave," says Three-Toed Sloth.

"Government has been made obsolete by Insurance," says Bumblebee.

"I'd rather starve than work for minimum wage," says Stork.

"The world would be better off if it were run by a computer," says Spider.

"The world is a computer," says Flu

"The world would be better off if it were overrun by grass," says Cow.

"The world would be better off if we each had our own world, which, come to think of it, we do, so why am I trying to change it," says Pigeon, who turns and starts walking away.

"You're trying to change YOUR world," says Catfish.

"Oh, right! Thanks for reminding me," he says, and returns to his booth.

"The first time the term 'crock of shit' was used was when Panda was presented with a crock that had been filled with shit and introduced to him as a crock of stew," says Hedgehog.

"Excuse me," said Panda, "but this is a crock of shit."

"And that," says Peccary, "is pure shit, an absolute and complete negation of the Truth, for, as we all know, Truth is Food and Food Truth, even if it's shit."

"I think god is a picture in my head," says Muskrat. "It's a scene which I don't think I've ever seen, yet somehow guides my life."

"Describe it for me," says Catbird.

"It's a market of some kind, and in the left foreground a group of people are talking. I have a feeling they're educators, and they have started cooperating, linking their subjects so students cannot complete their knowledge with one before being referred to another for the next stage of their education. In the right foreground is another group, more fractious and stern in demeanor, who look as if they will not compromise on their ideals, because each believes his own vision to be the one true vision, for which he'd die... but their potential followers are being monopolized by the other group, so they have agreed to come together, temporarily, for the purpose of defeating a common adversary."

"That's all in the picture," asks Catbird.

"It's a detailed picture," says Muskrat, and, after a pause, adds, "and almost lost in the business in the middle distance is Catfish and what looks like either a tall woodchuck or a fat beaver."

"I have a feeling someone's watching us," says Beaver.

"There is," says Catfish, "and she's walking straight toward us."

"God am I glad to see you," she says as she approaches.

"Do we know you," asks Beaver.

"I'm Cottontail," she says, "and I'm from your nick of the woods."

"I came here for work," says Cottontail, "because, like true love, I believe in callings, and I thought this place was calling me, but it's not working out, because everyone's too busy to tell me what I'm supposed to be doing, until I've done it wrong, and then they fire me, so I never have a chance to decide if I'm doing the right thing or not… and I'm running out of money."

"Wait," says Beaver, "are you trying to sell us something?"

"I don't know," says Cottontail, "Has anything I said sounded salable?"

"No," says Catfish.

"Well," says Cottontail, "then I'm not trying to sell you anything. But seriously," she says, "we need to get out of here before this place explodes."

She explains to them the impending bloodbath between the orthodoxists and the heterodoxists, as she has named the concerned parties, and begs them to board their ship and take her away with them.

"I don't buy it," says Beaver.

"We don't have to," says Catfish. "It's free."

They step aside and Beaver whispers to Catfish, "I see how you look at her."

"Maybe this is what I'm looking for," she says.

"Alright, but keep your eyes open," says Beaver.

So Muskrat travels back.

And Catbird joins him.

As they move over the darkening landscape, they both hear a muffled explosion inside Muskrat's head.

And the picture is a picture of carnage now.

A crater where thought was.

Hell's canary opens his eyes, flies to his perch, and begins to sing.

Outside the fair is the world.

Outside the world are the walls of a room.

Outside the room is hell.

Outside hell is Muskrat's heart.

Outside Muskrat's heart is Muskrat.

And Catbird shaking him, telling him to snap out of it.

Canary's song wakes Lamb.

He rises from his stone slab and stretches.

His chains fall away and he steps from his cell into the middle of the road.

Catbird screams.

Muskrat swerves off the road.

Bullfrog sings an inconsolable song of sorrow from atop an overturned car.

A dense fog rolls in, and out of it steps Lamb.

"Tell me of your sorrow," he says to Bullfrog. "And give me only the Truth, the story pure and unadorned."

"Mother died giving birth to me," sings Bullfrog, "and father used to beat me every day with an applewood switch.

"I left home young, to work on the railroad, and didn't return until, decades later, I received a letter informing me of my father's suicide.

"The house was much as I'd left it, with the exception that all traces of my mother and I had been removed, all traces but what I found on the top shelf of his bedroom closet, my mother's wedding dress, carefully folded, and, laying atop it, the applewood switch."

Bullfrog sings, "We are the living space, beaten into memory. We are the expansion of the past, where what is done is being done forever up to the instant of being, being being perpetual prelude to the past that is doing what is living space."

"Your song is second only to the birdsong of unbeing," says Lamb.

"Tell me," says Lamb, "where I might find those fornicators on whose wreck you sit, those who have given you this platform for song, for I am come of the realm of infinite potential, to find those who have diminished us with fire and shrapnel."

"They staggered that way, into the woods," says Bullfrog.

"Thank you," says Lamb, and, before Bullfrog can blink, Lamb separates Bullfrog's mind from his body, with the sword he keeps up his sleeve.

"So you will remain forever pure," explains Lamb, as he disappears into the wilderness.

Now Bullfrog blinks.

He lies in the mud.

Above him sits his body still, in the moonlight of another life.

Now Bullfrog sings to his body.

"'Concentrate,' the catbird had said, 'on the picture that used to be in your head.'

"'I see it now,' Muskrat replied, wiping blood from his eyes, 'some kind of rabbit turning her back on a suitcase in the middle foreground.'

"A rabbit talking now to Catfish and either a tall woodchuck or a fat beaver, on the deck of a small spacecraft approaching Earth."

"Come to my village," says Cottontail, "You'll be most welcome among my people."

"We would be honored," says Catfish, and Beaver grunts.

Muskrat sails down over the treetops, and in the distance, beside a river, a clearing appears, a translation of forest into clapboard houses and wood plank streets, outlined by a tall, watchtowered wall.

Outside the western wall grows a typical appendage of a town this age, a scattering of meager dwellings of the recently arrived, and their livestock.

And at the very edge of this eventual theater district lies a ramshackle, one-room hut that now serves as schoolhouse to the ancestors of some future middle class, and, peering through a rear window of this shack are Muskrat and Catbird, still bloodied, but once again in possession of their usual levels of consciousness.

At the front of the room stands Elephant, speaking to a class of bunnies.

"Now, children," she says, "I've heard rumors about what the substitute teacher taught you yesterday, things that would be enough to ensure she never taught in this town again, things that would ensure her descendants be reviled for generations to come, that they be exiled to the subterranean world of violent criminals and sexual deviants.

"Now," she says, "I want you to tell me exactly what she told you, including all the juicy bits."

The students stare blankly at Elephant.

"Don't sit there like idiots," says Elephant, "I want to hear about the sexual act, and I want to hear about it now!"

One of the students raises his hand.

"Very good," says Elephant. "Speak."

"Teacher said…"

"Substitute teacher," Elephant corrects.

"Substitute teacher said that a male and a female must come together in love in order for a healthy new life to be formed."

Elephant stares blankly at the student.

"I don't think you understand me," says Elephant. "I want the dirty stuff."

"My sister has infected toenails," blurts another student.

"No, god damn it," shouts Elephant. "I want you to tell me all the filthy, incriminating shit that Mule taught you yesterday! I want tittie-fucking, ass-packing, rim-splitting, three-cocks-in-your-mouth-and-one-in-your-ear confessions, and I want them now!"

The students stare blankly at Elephant.

One of them raises her hand and asks, "Um, mam, what is a 'rim'?"

"I think I've heard enough," announces a voice from the back of the room, and the congregation turns in unison to see Lamb standing in the doorway.

Lamb walks to the front of the room and decapitates Elephant.

Elephant's head knocks over several desks, with screaming children still seated in them, and her body slumps to its knees and sprays the interior of the room with the mighty crimson effulgence of Elephant's heart.

When the last ebb of life has throbbed from Elephant's neck, Lamb stands dripping before the students and says, "Today's lesson is over. In fact, that's about all you'll ever need to know. Go home and get to work.

"Oh, but before you go, tell me where those two terrorists are. I followed their trail to this building, so I know they've been through here. Come on, speak up… or I might get angry at injustice again."

The children's lesson is once again interrupted, this time by a blowhorn outside announcing that the school is surrounded and all perpetrators of unsanctioned violence must exit the building with empty hands raised in the air.

"You'll have to come in and get me," Lamb shouts.

"I'm sorry," the blowhorn says, "I can't hear you. Could you come to the open window and repeat that please?"

Lamb grabs one of the children and hauls her to the window where he holds his sword to the child's throat and shouts, "I'm not coming out till you hand over the terrorists!"

Swamp Rabbit, one of the volunteer sharpshooters, removes the sword from Lamb's hand with an exceedingly thoughtful shot.

The sword pinwheels into a tree.

Lamb pats his little hostage on the head and smiles at the crowd outside.

His feet and hands are put in irons.

Bloodied children file listlessly out of the schoolhouse like old prisoners.

Lamb now stands between two guards on a platform erected in the town square, before five graying hares in judicial robes and two eye witnesses: Muskrat and Catbird.

"Can I have a last cigarette," asks Lamb.

"No," says the senior judge, Mountain Hare, "but, because we are a civilized people, we will allow you to call an attorney of your choice to represent you."

Lamb calls Adder.

Adder's standing behind Lamb before Lamb even puts the phone to his ear.

"I'm right here," says Adder, and Lamb jumps.

Adder and Lamb confer quietly together, each taking turns nodding and whispering.

Then Adder turns from Lamb, to take advantage of a more theatrical angle, his good side to the judges and his better side to the crowd.

"Now," he announces, "I will explain to you how this most unfortunate of misunderstandings came to be."

"What the primary witnesses, who, incidentally, are of highly questionable character, as they are suspected terrorists…"

"Slander," shouts Muskrat.

"Please," says Mountain Hare. "Let us consider one case at a time."

"As I was saying, before the outburst," says Adder, "the witnesses have failed to tell us that when my client appeared on the scene, Elephant was in the process of indoctrinating her students into a cult of sexual perversion and criminal behavior, to which I'm sure the poor children will attest."

"It was horrible," cries a tiny adder in the crowd.

"Poor child," continues Adder. "The fact is that Elephant had the preexisting condition of a corrupt and deficient soul, which denied her coverage by the same laws that govern the rest of us in the moral universe. In fact, Elephant was never truly alive, in a moral sense. She was merely less dead, a mindless genetic vehicle.

"My client liberated her from her affliction." He pauses, as if in thought, and then continues.

"There are certain questions which we, the new and improved, still cannot answer, questions such as 'How can our individual essences be both different from, and alike, those of all others?', 'What's the difference between time and eternity?', 'Is pure narrative pure nonsense or pure poetry?', 'How can you prove that you're not dreaming right now?', and 'Why do distant things appear to be small?'

"We cannot yet dream of answering such subtle questions, but we can certainly answer this simple one: 'Did my client not save your children from the unspeakable violations of a ravenous sexual beast?'"

"Yes! Yes!" chants the crowd.

After the judges deliberate amongst themselves, Mountain Hare stands, quiets the crowd with an upheld hand, and announces, "We find the defendant innocent of all charges."

He then turns to Adder and asks, "Now, on what grounds do you accuse the witnesses of terrorism?"

At that exact moment, Cottontail appears at the front of the crowd, waving up at Mountain Hare and shouting, "Daddy! Daddy!"

Muskrat leaps to his feet and points at Cottontail. "That's her," he shouts. "She's the one who planted the bomb!"

Mountain Hare orders Jackrabbit, the head of security, to have the troublemakers escorted from town, and never allowed within the walls again.

As they are being marched away, Muskrat sees Catfish in the crowd and calls out to her.

Catfish hears her name and turns, but sees only a troop of soldiers leaving through the western gate.

"What are you looking at," asks Beaver.

"Nothing," she says. "It's just… I thought I heard a familiar voice… but it was nothing."

"Well, let's keep moving," he says. "I predict a party in our honor ahead."

Muskrat, Catbird, Lamb, and Adder sit on a log at the edge of the forest, facing the walled city.

"Listen to them sing," says Catbird. "You guys royally fucked it up for us."

"We could be living it up right now."

"I need to get back inside and find Catfish," says Muskrat.

"If you're right about that Cottontail, I need to get back in there myself," says Lamb.

"You guys are pathetic," says Catbird. "I said 'living it up,' not 'getting revenge' or whatever you call it."

"I think this is fun," says Adder.

In the morning, a large wooden carrot lies before the western gate.

Later, that evening, hungry and sick of sitting on top of one another, our four heroes emerge from a large pile of wooden rabbit droppings.

"Now how the hell do you suppose they did that," says Adder.

"Why are you still here," says Catbird.

"Because something smells fishy," says Adder, "and that's where I come in."

"And what court is going to try the case," she says.

"Let me worry about that," says Lamb.
"Be my guest."
"We should find some shelter," says Muskrat. "It's starting to snow."

"It's starting to snow," says Cottontail, joining Catfish on the balcony of her father's mansion. "Would you like to come inside?"
"Not yet," says Catfish. "I like the snow."

She stands there, staring out over the city wall, at a wilderness disappearing into the falling snow and dark.

"That barren tree," she says, "down there, branches like a neural network, roots a mirror network below the earth, trunk an axial bridge between the two, is which the brain and which the throbbing body, which burrowing into the light of thought and which rising into the darkness of sensation, which growing out of which, which birds are in those branches, which bodies in those roots, which minds in that mind…"

"You're alright," Cottontail says, gently touching her arm.

"I feel like there's a keyhole in my side," says Catfish, "and I'm slipping through it, little by little, into an unknown world, on the other side of an unknown door. I don't think I'm here anymore."

"Please don't say that," says Cottontail. "Stay with me. Tell me how you got on the moon."

"My friend Fox asked me to visit him and his girlfriend Mink at her home up north. He wanted me to observe them. He said he thought she was acting strange, but he wanted an objective opinion.

"I found them at the end of the northern road.

"We went for a long walk, starting from where the road stopped.

"Mink showed us her favorite apple tree and picked us each an apple.

"As we walked, a bat swooped in front of us and I flinched in surprise.

"Fox chuckled.

"Mink said incest was common in her tribe.

"I flinched again and said, 'Now?'

"'Yes,' she said, 'everyone is always drinking, and when they're drunk they do things that no one ever talks about, and it will never stop until they start talking about it, but they think it's worse to talk about it than to do it, but I'm going to start talking about it one of these days, and then the shit will hit the fan!'

"Fox walked quietly ahead of us.

"When we got back we got drunk in the kitchen.

"Fox produced a bag of blow and we each did a couple lines.

"'When is this shit gonna kick in,' said Mink.

"'It's pure,' said Fox. 'Chill out.'

"'Or what,' Mink demanded, 'you'll beat my ass again?'

"'Oh please,' said Fox, 'not in front of my friend.'

"'I think she should know what kind of friend you really are.'

"'Go ahead,' she said to me. 'Ask him why he threw me on the ground. Ask him why he kicked me in my implants.'

"'No way, that's not what happened!'

"'The hell it isn't!'

"'Oh jesus,' I whispered.

"'I hate sex,' she screamed, 'because that's all he wants, and when he doesn't get it, he beats me!'

"'That's not true,' he shouted. 'Why don't you tell her how you punched me in the face? And why don't you tell her why you really hate sex? Why don't you tell her how you were raped in the ass by your uncle when you were a kid!'

"'You're the one who rapes me,' she screamed. 'You're raping me right now, in front of your fucking friend!'

"'Fuck you!'

"'No, fuck you!'

"As they screamed back and forth, I clutched my head in my hands to stifle the pounding.

"I saw an aspirin bottle on the counter and shook several pills out and swallowed them.

"It got worse.

"My heart began beating so fast I couldn't count the beats.

"My vision blurred and the room quieted, and then, as if from far away, I heard Fox's voice.

"He said, 'Did you just take a bunch of my Adderall?'

"I sat down right where I was standing.

"I closed my eyes.

"I knew I could die unless I focused all of my awareness on my heart and talked it down.

"I pushed the whole earth away from my heart.

"I watched it recede into the starry distance.

"I was standing on the moon now."

Mink puts a blanket over Catfish's shoulders and retreats to the couch, where she sits and watches.

Fox crouches beside Catfish, taking her pulse every ten minutes.

"Is she alright," Mink asks.

After a while, Fox joins Mink on the couch.
"How is she," Mink asks.
"I think she's meditating," he says.

After a while, they help her to the couch.
Mink goes to bed, and Fox falls asleep in a chair beside the couch.
The house is perfectly quiet the rest of the night.

The next morning, there's a knocking at the door.
Mink gets it, in her bathrobe.
Muskrat and Beaver stand in the doorway shivering.

"What do you want," she says.
"Is Catfish here," asks Muskrat.
"Come in," she says.

"She's lying on the couch. She had a rough night. We all did."

"It's nice she has someone who would drive up here looking for her," says Mink. "I don't."
"You don't what," asks Fox, entering the foyer.

"What's up dog," says Beaver.
Mink leaves the room.
Muskrat goes to the couch.

"Been better," says Fox.
Muskrat helps Catfish to her feet and leads her to the foyer.
"We're going home," he says.

"I'm sorry things turned out the way they did," says Fox.

"No problem," says Catfish. "It helped me put things in perspective."

They embrace and part.

Mink rejoins Fox and Beaver in the living room.

"I hate being around happy couples," she says.

"Lucky you," says Fox.

"Did I ever tell you why my band broke up," asks Beaver, "why we exiled ourselves from the garden of our own creation?"

"I didn't know you were in a band," says Fox.

"For a couple years after college."

"When I was dealing meth in Minneapolis?"

"Right… we visited you once."

"Oh."

"We broke up after our third tour.

"The first was our 'East Coast Tour,' followed by our 'West Coast Tour,' and we were calling the third our 'Known World Tour.'

"We agreed to always keep a Great Lake on the right side of the van.

"After we'd booked all the shows, Eel's girlfriend threw us a launch party.

"And the next morning we hit the road to The North.

"Somewhere in Skokie, Monkey announced he was tripping too hard to drive anymore.

"No one heard him because we were all sleeping, and because, he later admitted, he'd maybe only said it in his head, so he exited 94, and, some time in the afternoon, I woke to a chorus of snoring and a fly pirouetting on the tip of my nose.

"'Are we there,' I asked.

"'They're married,' Eel mumbled, and the snoring continued.

"I crawled over Otter and slid open the side door.

"Sunlight and the odor of warm blacktop filled my head up to eternity.

"We were at the edge of a busy Walmart parking lot, in the middle of anywhere in the known world, and there, about twenty feet away, smiling from ear to ear, squatting over a growing pile of his own crap, was Monkey.

"He waved to me.

"I waved back.

"We missed our first gig in somebody's basement in Milwaukee that evening, and I confiscated Monkey's acid.

"We called ourselves *Gnarly Wounds*, and we were Eel on guitar, Otter on bass, Monkey on drums, and yours truly on mic.

"For every show the band jammed extempore, and I chanted lyrics I'd written earlier that day.

"'That was our shtick.'"

"I'm making coffee," says Mink. "Would you like some?"

"Sure," says Beaver, "with a splash of cream please."

"Is milk acceptable?"

"Sure."

"I'd like a cup as well," says Fox, "strong and black."

"Would you," she says.

"Monkey was like that," says Beaver.

"Eel was self-consciously cool. He'd get wound up tighter and tighter throughout the day, till we turned on the amps. Then he'd release it all in a barrage of tightly controlled dissonance.

"Otter was unconsciously cool, like myself I liked to think. I also thought I was in love with her, but I was married, and she wasn't into men, so I kept it to myself.

"She played her bass like a lover, and when she spoke, she told you what was what.

"She was one of those people that're so deep they have no surface.

"When she touched you, you could feel the weight of her whole life behind the touch."

"Sounds like love," says Mink, handing them each a mug.

"Thanks," says Beaver.

"You're too kind," says Fox.

Fox stares out the window at the clear sky and the darkest shadows the sun can cast. And in the space of the following breath, nothing moves within that scene, and he feels this space expand to fill the space beyond all their lives.

The shadow is what was always there, before the trees and the light, he thinks.

"Monkey wasn't the reason we missed our first show," says Beaver.

"We could have made it if someone else had gotten behind the wheel and hauled ass, but I'd said no.

"I'd had a terrible dream full of screams and blood and ideology in the back of that van, and I needed to rethink our whole tour.

"I announced that I couldn't perform any material I'd written before I fell asleep.

"I needed to start over.

"I needed to set something straight.

"'What is it,' Otter wanted to know.

"'I can't tell you until I've got it on paper,' I said.

"'Whatever,' said Eel, 'I'll drive.'

"In Green Bay, I unveiled the first of the new lyrics.

"Monkey gave us a drum roll, Eel struck a prehistoric chord, Otter put the earth under our feet.

"And I spent the next forty five minutes assembling and disassembling and reassembling, word by word, phrase by phrase, backwards and forwards and inside out, the following:

"My sister delivered a twelve inch sausage pizza to the abortion clinic.

"When she left, a man screamed at her.

"'You have no right to choose,' the man screamed, 'for the lord is the only one who has a choice, and the lord almighty doesn't kill babies anymore.'

"As we drove farther north and the number of pickup trucks increased, so did the dread my dream had awakened in me.

"No one in the band had commented on my new style, until we'd pulled over at a rest stop so Monkey could take a dump and Eel could call his girlfriend.

"Otter and I sat at a picnic table in the sun, between the parking lot and the restrooms.

"'I don't usually listen to your lyrics,' said Otter, 'but last night I did.'

"'Why's that,' I said.

"'You don't usually sound like you believe what you're saying, like you're just saying it because that's what people expect from you.

"'And sometimes it sounds really cool,' she said, 'but it doesn't go anywhere, doesn't accomplish anything, doesn't even describe your feelings any better than your stage presence does.'

"'So you think we're making a real difference.'

"'I'm saying that the reason I listened last night is because you finally sounded like you actually believed what you were saying.'

"'Last night, the clash between your ridiculous lyrics and your passionate delivery created a wave that I, for one, was trying to surf.

"'It's like we were starting to deconstruct the tired old dualities of form and content, thought and feeling, culture and instinct, gender and sex… langue and parole…

"'I think we've made a stylistic breakthrough,' she said.

"'You think the lyrics were ridiculous,' I said.

"'In a way,' she said, 'and repetitive.'

"'But I feel strongly about them,' I said. 'I had a dream.'

"'Of course you did,' she said, 'and that's cool.'

"'But if I believe in something ridiculous, don't you think that makes me ridiculous?'

"'You'd only be truly ridiculous if you didn't care what I thought.'

"'So, as long as I care what you think, I can say whatever I want.'

"'Theoretically. But let's play it by ear a bit longer, before we come to any conclusions.'

"In Duluth we played a warehouse, under a bridge, under the stars.

"The full moon swam in our blood like it does in a cool deep well.

"I sang over and under and through:

My sister delivered a malpractice policy to the abortion clinic.
"When she left, a man slapped her across the face.
"'Experience is a sin,' he screamed, 'You must stay pure forever, or you must forever die.'

"Monkey disappeared in Thunder Bay.
"We played an abandoned garage and partied with appreciative Canadians in a dump at the edge of town.
"A flock of prehistoric shapes flew across the dawn.

"Otter woke me around noon.
"We'd been sleeping on the floor of one of the Canadians' apartments.
"'Monkey's gone,' she said.

"'Monkey likes parks,' I said. 'Let's check out the local parks.'
"'He was talking to Skunk at the dump,' said the Canadian.
"Skunk didn't answer his phone, so Eel and the Canadian went in search of Skunk.

"Walking through Vickers Park, Otter said, 'Why is Monkey always fucking up our plans?'
"'He's the youngest of us,' I said. 'He probably doesn't feel like he's got any responsibilities.'
"'Must be nice,' she said. 'I wish I'd had an older sibling, or one at all.'

"'If it doesn't weird you out,' I said, 'you can think of me as your older brother. I sort of already think of you as my little sister. Does that bother you?'

"'No,' she said. 'It feels good. It explains a lot.'

"Eel found Monkey and Skunk sleeping naked in Skunk's car.
"Neither of them could remember where their clothes were.
"They stumbled into Skunk's building, and we followed.

"They took their time dressing in Skunk's room.
"The Canadian nuked some instant coffee for us.
"When they finally emerged from Skunk's room, Monkey was wearing Skunk's clothes.

"They drank coffee with us.
"And, for the first time I can remember, Monkey seemed calm and almost mature.
"We said goodbye and hit the road to our next gig.

"'My sister delivered a bouquet of day lilies and baby's breath to the abortion clinic,' I sang.
"When she left, a man punched her in the face and screamed, 'Touching is evil. Touching the flesh in love or hate or desperation must be punished. Now look what you made me do!'

"In Sault Saint Marie, Otter and I snuck away for a couple hours in the afternoon, while Eel and Monkey were setting up their equipment.
"We walked along the locks, in a warm breeze smelling of winter.
"We sat on a bench and watched a tanker slowly sink out of sight in a lock before us.

"'I think I'm attracted to you,' she said, 'and I think I've always been.'
"'I think I've known,' I said, 'and I've felt the same. But I've made myself think of you as a sister these past years, and now it feels strange to think of you any other way.'

"'Why don't you ever call your wife,' she said.

"'We're alive,' I said. 'What more do we need.'

"'Much more,' she said.

"'My sister delivered seventy million tons of greenhouse gases to the abortion clinic,' I sang that night.

"When she left, a man kicked her in the stomach, and when she fell to the sidewalk, he kicked her over and over, shouting, 'I can't believe in a world I can't feel pounding against my literal flesh! My faith is my fist!'

"In Sudbury, we had to physically extricate Monkey from an establishment fondly referred to by locals as the 'Crack Shack.'

"And Otter said, 'We can't do anything about it, can we.'

"And I said, 'I don't think of myself as straight or gay, but as living among the living, loving sometimes their words and sometimes their eyes.'

"In Toronto, Eel broke down. 'I can't take this shit anymore,' he screamed, 'trying to keep Monkey from killing himself, while you two are off doing whatever! I'm a musician, goddamnit, a living, breathing musician!'

"'I know,' I said. 'You're the heart of the band… the heart…'

"'That's right,' he said.

"'Don't you forget it,' I said.

"We kissed in Humber Bay Park, after the show, after the equipment was stowed, after Monkey and Eel were well into their cups.

"We slipped away, to the numberless plane of the lake.

"Her breath, her lips, her tongue, the smell of her filling me.

"In London, in an alley, she pinned me against the bricks.

"'Say you fucking love me,' she said.
"I said.

"Between the stars are propositions not spoken yet, not whispered in the dark of a vessel, after everyone else has drifted off, maybe a hundred miles from the next motel, under bridges, behind tree lines, behind concrete sound barriers erected at the edge of mumbling freeways.

"Before the windshield was our past.

"Before it seethed an impenetrable tangle of vines and tails and fins and tentacles and thorns and claws.

"Monkey was passed out in the back seat in his own vomit.

"Eel had demanded out, and had disappeared on foot, into a freak snowstorm.

"'I feel love, but I don't feel joy, the joy of your body,' she said. 'What we have is too heavy, too serious, like we're fighting death instead of succumbing to life.'

"'I've really tried,' she said, 'but I just don't think I can be with a man.'

"'Uh huh,' I said.

"'Pee,' said Monkey.

"I watched a silhouette shift and turn and turn again in the falling snow.

"I wanted it to erupt into a bird of flame and disappear into the night sky, but it turned into Eel and he pounded on the windshield. 'I'm not getting back in until you've cleaned him up!'

"So I cleaned him up.

"I hauled him out of the van, onto his back in the ditch, and stripped him naked.

"I threw all his clothes into the storm, except for his sweatshirt, which I used to wipe his piss and puke off the vinyl seats. Then I wound up and threw that into oblivion as well.

"He'd gotten back to his feet and staggered toward me, pale as the snow, crying, 'No, not Skunk. Don't take Skunk away from me...'

"'Shut the fuck up,' I yelled. 'You know you're never gonna see him again! You know it, you know it, you pathetic shit!'

"I pushed him to the ground and knelt over him, scrubbing him with fistfuls of snow while he sobbed.

"When I couldn't feel my hands anymore, I stopped.
"There was a hand on my shoulder.
"'It's okay,' said Eel. 'We better get him inside now.'

"In Detroit, we were each alone on the stage together.
"Music oozed from us.
"Words ran down my chin.

"My sister delivered a suitcase containing forty pounds of plastic explosive and nails to the abortion clinic.

"When she left, everyone left, the doctor, the nurse, the receptionist, the knocked-up knock-kneed teenager, the knocked-up knock-kneed teenager's mother, the unborn existentialist, the man who was waiting for my sister with a knife this time, the woman holding to her chest a lurid image of what they would all become, her son beside her, a boy of twelve, dreaming of tits and ass.

"'Look,' he said, and then they were gone.

"The snow turned pale brown as we entered the city limits of Gary.

"All about us factories exchanged smoke and fire with the heavens.

"This was to be our last show.

"When it was our turn, we set up, tested our equipment, and stood there, staring at a common point on the floor between us, where nothing was.

"Finally, Monkey spoke. 'I'm ready now.'

"'I can play forever,' he said.

"Eel nodded to me.

"Otter looked me in the eyes, heavy as ever, and I said, 'Okay then, let's do it:

When Catbird was sixteen, she told her mom she wanted to live with her dad because her friends all lived in the town where he was, and her mom sat her down and poured them each a glass of wine.

"I'm willing to let you go," her mother said, "but first I want you to know your father's secret. When you were a child, he was arrested several times, for lewd and lascivious behavior."

"You mean when he screwed around on you?"

"Don't be silly. They don't arrest people for that."

"Your father used to put on a ski mask and masturbate in front of people's patio doors." She took drink of her wine. "And he got caught. So, for a while, after dropping you off at daycare, I'd pick your father up at the county jail and drive him to work, and I'd bring him back to jail between getting off from my job and picking you up at daycare. I had to do that off and on for a couple years, until he kicked the habit… or stopped getting caught."

"Oh my god," Catbird said, "now I understand why you divorced him."

"Don't be silly," her mother said. "I divorced him because he screwed around on me."

"I'm so sorry, Mom."

"Mom?"

"Yes?"

"Please don't tell Dad I know."

So Catbird moved in with her father and his fourth wife.

And, for a time, she had the time of her life.

Then she fell ass-over-teakettle in love, for the first and last time she thought, with her friend Raccoon…who proceeded to disappear with her slutty friend Crayfish, and a couple months later she found out, through a friend-of-a-friend, that they were living together in a friend-of-a-friend's pool house in Los Angeles.

Then Muskrat shows up heartbroken at the door of her mother's cabin, and she decides to stop waiting for love.

She steps, stripped to her leather tunic, from her tent, into the faint ember glow of one of the countless campfires that ring the walled city of the rabbits.

Now the host of gods and heroes slumber, but the grip of sleep holds not Canary, perched in immortality's grey chamber, turning over in his mind how to exult Catbird.

"Though you have grown to be the greatest warrior among us, I know you fear death as well," says an old cur, sitting alone by the fire, "but fear not your own, for beyond the river of stars and the known and the felt is the imagined world, where you shall be a god."

"Thanks for the pep talk, grampa," says Catbird, "but I'm more concerned about having my head dunked in napalm if I'm captured."

"I'm just saying," says grampa.

Into the hissing circle of light steps Adder.

"Is that why you fight like the devil," he says, "for fear of pain?"

"In a sense," she says. "What brings you?"

"I bear a message."

"Go on."

"Lamb has had a dream, and in the dream he looked into the river and was astonished to see that he was a large rodent, and his bowels began to ache, and he squatted with his arms around a tree and strove with all his might to disgorge the contents of his bowels, but he could not, though he pushed till his vision clouded, and he heard a voice speak to him, and the voice said, 'You shall not prevail against Ileus until you believe with the purity and the hatred of an infant.'"

"You're going to have to help me with that one."

"Okay, I'll be blunt. We believe we're making no progress against the infidels because there are those among us who fight without belief or conviction, and, though your prowess on the field implies a powerful faith, we seek reassurance that nihilism has found no purchase among our leaders."

"Who's 'we'?"

"Lamb, Muskrat, and myself."

"Muskrat?"

"Yes, he too."

"Tell him I fight because I said I would, because I gave him my word."

"Our hold is too tenuous to risk the wrath of the unspeakable. We ask for the higher purpose of your slaughter."

"You want me to make something up?"

"You miss my point."

"Well then I'm afraid I can't help you."
"But it's such a simple thing, to simply believe in something."

"Look, even if I did, I wouldn't demean my belief by producing it upon demand, like some kind of ticket. You either need my help or you don't."
"I didn't come here to feed your ego."
"Then I guess my ego will stay lean, for I'll fight no more for you."

"I'll let you in on a little secret," she says. "Every world is the same to one who is outside all worlds."
"But you need not be," he says. "You need only choose a faith, any faith."
"Good night," she says, nods to the old cur by the fire, and disappears into her tent.

"The bird's got a point," says the old cur.
"And so do I," says Adder.
"Ay," says the old cur, "there's the rub."

Adder slips back into the night.
The old cur yawns and goes back to sleep.
And all around the city, the armies of dog sleep.

In the cold mist before sunrise, Catbird goes down to the river and stands on the wet sand of the shore.
"Mother," she says quietly, "what should I do? My word is my life and my word is my death, and my word isn't enough for him anymore… but I cannot leave, because I gave him my word, pure and true."

And up rises Otter, glistening, from the water, and stands before Catbird.

"My poor child," she says, "I hope it wasn't I who gave you this unyielding heart, who turned the world to stone beneath your feet."

She envelopes Catbird in her arms and says, "Sleep, sleep my dearest, soften your will with dreams, and I will do what I can to bring him to his knees."

The rabbits bring ruin down on the dogs that day.

The great field marshal, Jackrabbit, clad in black Kevlar, machete flashing, leaps their earthworks and hacks passage into the dogs' front lines.

He visits misery on many.

After Jackrabbit's visit, Dalmatian drops to his knees, arterial blood christening his comrades.

Husky gazes down on the battle as her head floats high through the air, and she thinks, "Ah, from this perspective it makes some kind of sense," before the dark veil is drawn over her eyes.

Water Spaniel glances down at his bowels, glistening in the mud, and says, "Hello!"

Lamb takes an arrow in the kneecap and pitches forward into blasphemies.

Muskrat is knocked unconscious by a concussion grenade.

Later, he wakes to a light rain rustling the bloody earth and bodies, in the silence behind the rabbit's line.

"Perhaps I'm wrong," he thinks. "Perhaps this isn't love. Perhaps this is only what it appears to be."

Soon the dogs are pressed to the edge of the forest, where they barely manage to hold their ground, firing from behind the trees.

The dogs fight like never before, because now they fight for nothing but their lives.

"Oh," cries Mutt, "that only Catbird were with us now, leading a lusty charge against these bloodthirsty rodents!"

Adder runs, under cover of the trees, a wide circuit round the clamoring battle, to the far side where Catbird's tents stand, and he bursts in on her and falls to his knees and implores her to return to the field in all her murderous glory.

"I'm nobody's whore," she says. "Tell them to unsheathe their precious beliefs now."

The sun slips behind the hills, and the war cries diminish.

The world reclines into a temporary moaning.

Fires are lit, and the shadows of great birds play at the margins of dusk.

Eel steps from the shadows at the end of a hallway in Mountain Hare's mansion.

He enters Mountain Hare's study.

Mountain Hare looks up from his charts and says, "My god, I thought I would never see you again."

They walk unnoticed through the city, out the southern gate, through the twilight aftermath of murder, and into Lamb's tent.

Lamb looks up from his bandages, and his grimace of pain is replaced by astonishment.

Eel nods to Mountain Hare, and Mountain Hare says quietly, "Let God decide who is guilty in a hand to hand trial between my daughter and her accuser."

"Hot damn," says Lamb, "You're on! Tomorrow morning, in the field before the southern gate!"

He turns and yells through the tent flap, "Adder, find Muskrat, and get that boy some dinner!"

When he turns back, his guests are gone.

Morning finds Muskrat and Cottontail facing one another, knives in hand, across an expanse of knee-high grass, a wall of weary soldiers behind each.

"Is this your idea of love," she says.

"It seemed right at the time."

"No matter who wins, your army will leave," says Cottontail, "but She will still do as she pleases."

"Nothing will stop me from trying," he says.

"You sad, silly creature," she says, "have you ever considered talking to her?"

"Shut up and fight," shouts a dog.

"Yeah," shouts a rabbit, "we've got things to do."

"Lives to return to," shouts another.

Cottontail shrugs and rushes at Muskrat, her blade flashing like fire above her head.

Muskrat kicks her in the throat, and she falls flat on her back, gasping, her blade fallen into the grass.

Muskrat straddles her and puts his knife to her throat.

"I'm sorry," he says, "but I know of no other way to end."

And a shot rings out, and Muskrat blinks a couple times and slides sideways into the grass.

"Oops," says someone on the rabbit's side.

Time stops.

Monkey strolls down the corridor between the two armies.

He places his hands on either side of Muskrat's head and draws down the eyelids with his thumbs. Then he turns and takes Cottontail up in his arms.

He brings her to Catfish's chamber, lays her down beside Catfish, and leaves the room.

Time resumes.

"I have to leave now," says Catfish, and Cottontail says, "I understand, but I will miss you more than I can say."

And outside, two great waves of life crash together with renewed vengeance.

And Muskrat's body is lost beneath the surface.

He dreams he is swimming up a great river.

When Otter enters her tent, Catbird already has all her possessions of the ten-year campaign packed into a single duffle bag, and she sits on her cot with the bag on her lap and her face buried in her hands.

"Are you ready, my child," says Otter.

"I could have stopped him," Catbird mumbles.

"He has been stopped."

"That's not what I mean."

"I have done as you requested, and now it's my duty to bring you to the next movement," and she takes Catbird by the hand, and Catbird rises, and they step from the tent.

Into Mountain Hare's backyard, where *Muskrat* stands in a fine drizzle.

Catfish is embracing Cottontail, saying, "I'll never forget you."

Beaver, standing on the boarding ramp, nods to Otter, and calls out, "All aboard who wish to move on!"

Catfish and Catbird ascend the ramp and take seats in the cabin, on either side of Beaver.

They neither speak nor acknowledge each other's presence.

Muskrat ascends into the abstract and disappears from sight.

"I'm not traveling in silence," says Beaver. "The two of you must reconcile your loss. You still have much to be thankful for."

"You can be thankful that tyranny is merely the result of the fear of being reduced to nothingness, which doesn't exist, so no one can be reduced to it.

"You can be thankful that enlightenment leads to democracy which leads to endless bickering which leads to tyranny which leads to submission which leads to darkness which leads to enlightenment.

"You can be thankful that evil usually prevails over good only because people believe it will, because they have defined it more clearly than they have defined good.

"You can be thankful that the source of evil is the denial of love.

"That good and evil and love and hate exist only if you think they do.

"That the endless piling up of irrelevant details proves that you actually exist.

"You can be thankful your pain is felt by no one else.

"And if you aren't thankful for this, you can be thankful you understand the pain of others.

"That there are no bad people, just bad ideas… really bad ideas.

"You can be thankful you don't have to be thankful.

"That you've got a warm place to sleep, enough food to eat, and shoes on your feet.

"That you've got a job that doesn't make you hate yourself, like when you were selling insurance.

"That you're wife behaved in such a civil manner when you separated that it made you wonder if you'd made a horrible mistake.

"That the doctors tell you the tumor is benign.

"That the entire world is not a poisonous stew in which you cook.

"You can be thankful that thousands of years will pass and nothing will change more than you.

"You can be thankful we just ran out of gas and we're not in outer space."

Muskrat chuckles, is silent, and begins to slowly accelerate toward the earth.

"Whatever," says Catbird, and they all put on their seat belts.

The ship plows into a marsh and buries itself to the windshield in mud and cattails, and they sit and watch in silence as three thousand years flow around them.

A blue streak of weather gradually disassembles their ship, and humans stream across the horizon singing and crying and squatting in the switchgrass, and the land is drained and flattened into fields and paths and raised again into monuments of human dwelling and toiling and consuming and healing and risking and ruling and raising the earth into monuments, and our heroes now find themselves sitting on a couch in a tiny basement apartment that was built around them, watching human feet stream past the window overhead.

You can be thankful the sun still burns.

It still shows you the way home, when you've crawled from the airtight chemical bowels of the printing house.

As you walk, you feel it pulsing through your blood.

At home, you find Beaver, Catfish, and Catbird sitting on your couch.

"Do I know you," you say.

"You better believe it," says Beaver.

"We need your help," says Catfish.

"I'd love to help you," you say, "but my daughter's going to be here in half an hour, so you should probably leave."

"You have a daughter," says Catfish.

"Yes, and her mother's dropping her off, so I can take her to the zoo."

"The zoo," says Catbird. "How quaint."

"We're looking for Muskrat," says Beaver, "and if anyone knows where he is, it's you."

"I honestly can't help," you say. "I've successfully contained, in a place outside my head, everything that has haunted me, and now I'm free."

"Nice try," says Catbird, "but the story's not good enough to be done. Where's Muskrat?"

"Ah, yes," you say, "now I remember. I saw a muskrat scurry up the fire escape ladder from this apartment only minutes ago, when I was approaching the building…"

And he is hotly pursued by Catbird, Beaver, and Catfish, who, even as you speak, catch the scent of his trail and are out the window, up the fire escape, and down the alley before you can say goodbye.

"Goodbye," you say.

Night falls.

The stars catch it.

Snow falls on the living and the dead and the Warehouse Liquor across the street.

A child catches it on her tongue.
Muskrat falls.
He struggles to his feet and staggers on.

"Who was Muskrat," you ask.
He seemed defined merely by the motion of his body toward another.
And now the tide moves out.

Motion reverses.
Character shifts, yet the landscape remains the same.
They lose his trail and spread out into the city.

They lose their sense of time.
They lose their sense of smell.
They lose touch with one another.

In short, they get lost in the modern world.
They tune into the life of the times.
They find it hard to concentrate because now they know the NASDAQ is at a four year low and Paris Hilton doesn't wear underwear.

Because she's got an eye for detail, Catbird is offered a quality assurance job at a medical software company that squats like a temple on a hilltop at the edge of town.
She's paid to sit in an office all day and try to find flaws in their applications, so that, they say, fewer people will die.
What these people do after they fail to die she doesn't know.

Perhaps they go back to crack and beating their children with ball peen hammers.
Perhaps they find God and write inspirational verse.
She doesn't know. They don't have these kinds of statistics yet.

One day, a young man appears at her door and asks if she knows how to set up VMware, because he can't figure it out, and he needs it to start his certification project.

He's a serious type, but courteous, anxiously focused on a goal he clearly never imagined he'd have to achieve in life.

He reminds her of someone else who once came to her door, someone whose memory fills her now with remorse.

Beaver gets a job at Ballbuster Video.

He decides that the best way to support his search for Muskrat is to buy a no-money-down, fixer-upper on the industrial east side, put everything he makes into fixing it up, and sell it for a hearty profit when the neighborhood starts to gentrify.

He gets to step one and can't go any further, because, after making mortgage, utility, and insurance payments each month, he's got nothing left.

Shortly after this realization, his real estate experience becomes defined by an ongoing struggle with the municipal garbage collectors.

It starts with several barrels of soggy, decomposing yard waste, writhing with maggots, that were left in the garage by the previous owners, "two college chicks," says the one neighbor who speaks to him.

He wonders about this.

When he viewed the house, only one of the bedrooms was being used as a bedroom, while the other was clearly being used as a study.

There was only one bed in the house.

"After you made an offer on the place, one of them split for California," says the neighbor. "I don't know what happened to the other one."

"She seemed pretty shook up when we signed the papers," says Beaver. "I think she said something about going away to grad school."

The garbage collectors leave a note on one of the barrels of rot, informing Beaver that all yard refuse must be transported to the proper yard waste disposal locations by the owners of the properties from whence said refuse originates.

Beaver can hardly fit himself into his Geo Metro, so he has no idea how it would accommodate several barrels of stench, if he were even inclined to ask it to do so.

Beaver devises an alternate plan.

He puts on gloves and manually redistributes the waste into half-a-dozen heavy-duty garbage bags, into which he also deposits a healthy dose of non-yard waste, thereby disguising the true nature of the bags' contents, and deceiving the collectors into collecting what their beloved city prohibits the collection thereof.

And while he's up to his elbows in the putrescence, Beaver imagines the sad-eyed girl from the signing making love, in his bedroom, to a woman that would soon leave her.

He leaves the bags on the curb in the morning, and when he comes home from work they're gone.

In such manner, the city also unwittingly assumes possession of a dehumidifier, which the collectors inform Beaver will cost him nearly a day's wages to collect.

The dehumidifier is disassembled in the garage and redistributed into heavy-duty garbage bags, amidst other less refusable refuse, and is converted from private to public interest, in the manner, once again, of the lovers' legacy.

Beaver takes a guilty pride in his deceitfully simple solution.

To atone for this pride, Beaver takes in a stray cat who has been begging for food in the neighborhood.

Over the course of the year, the cat produces over one hundred pounds of dirty litter, which, Beaver soon discovers, the city wants him to bury in his backyard.

Beaver has no backyard.

Etcetera.
Etcetera.
Etcetera.

Though Beaver never actually sees the act of collection, he can recognize a pattern, whether he sees it or not.

It's either gone when he gets home, or it's waiting for him with a note.

He's always at work when it happens, usually helping someone find either *The Wizard of Oz* or *Swallow the Leader*.

Beaver comes home one evening and is ecstatic to see that his garbage has been collected.

He tosses the mail on the kitchen table and sits down to take off his shoes.

Pickle, his cat, jumps on his lap, and, as he absentmindedly pets the purring beast, he says, "Pickle, I can't shake the feeling that I'm forgetting something, that something has been collected that I hadn't wanted to be rid of."

Catfish doesn't forget.

She searches endlessly.

She starts specializing in "scenes," particularly openings, because these are the places, she has become convinced, from which people are reborn.

She's at a gallery opening tonight.

She makes the rounds, looking for him in every face.

She pauses before a canvas titled "A Soul in the World" and looks for him in the layers of paint, for he may have been someone else's subject too.

Eventually she goes home with an artist who is intrigued by her intensity.

On the way out the door, she brushes against an eel who is entering.

He glances at her over his shoulder and grins.

And then we have "Catfish in a Strange Bed."

She rises effortlessly, as if from a river bed, disturbing not the man beside her.

She dresses silently, takes a twenty from the wallet on the floor, and descends onto the street.

In the pale moonlight between street lamps she pauses.

A dog sleeps on the worn earth at the end of its chain, while several feet away a rabbit nibbles on a dandelion.

"Look at you," she whispers to them. "What has become of you?"

Catfish walks through morning.

Through what man has made and unmade and hasn't noticed since it first called itself man.

She comes across a broken cage, below the loading dock behind a university laboratory, and she watches a dozen white mice run terrified circles in the sunlight.

She walks through a foundry, where the iron hearts of stars are poured into the shapes of man, where one places a finger to the side of his nose and blows a string of iridescent snot to the earth where it steams.

She walks through a nuclear power plant and, pausing beside the reactor chamber, looks down into a pool of water that deepens from the lightest, softest blue to the brooding blue of afterbirth, in which she sees canisters stacked, and a man in white pauses beside her and looks down with her and says, "If you jumped in and started swimming toward the bottom, you'd be dead before you got there."

She walks through Weasel's Northwoods Burlesque, where a naked woman runs across stage, leaps into a room full of men wearing snowmobile suits, and lands on one with such force that he totters backwards in his chair and nearly falls over, and the woman pays no heed, but takes his head between her hands and, by a powerful and repeated torsion of her waist, pummels his face with her breasts. The crowd roars with approval.

She walks through time.
She is equal in time to the world that contains her.
She can't tell if time is tugging her through her life, heartbeat by heartbeat, or if it is merely clearing a path for her.

She walks through a park, pauses, and looks up.
Contrails have crossed in the sky, audacious as Constantine's cross…becoming lesser so the longer she watches.
A figure sits on a bench, spying on the world from behind the news.

After Catfish passes, the figure folds the paper, tucks it under an arm, and follows her.
She walks under a billboard on which float the smiling heads of an elephant and a donkey.
In a speech balloon, they once announced, "TERRORISM ISN'T PARTISAN," but now, under the influence of spraypaint, they gleefully shout, "TERRORISM JISMS PARTISANS!"

The figure follows.
It wears the trench coat and fedora you'd expect it to wear.
It deposits the paper in the proper trash receptacle as it passes.

Catfish walks through men upon men upon pavement upon bicycles upon horses upon the seats of motorized vehicles upon air.
Through the smoke of flesh and metal and plastic and wood and bone becoming smoke.
She walks.

Through great audiences of learning and unlearning.
The intestines of great reptiles digesting in the sunny reeds at water's edge.
Through fanatical passion for invention, and subsequent death and mayhem, she walks without pausing.

Through a tree line in the rain.
Dark interior music.
Antique air of forgotten rooms.

Through a fragrance of DNA born on the liquid of the wind.
The perversion of a truth that leads to a child being buried alive in the quiet, fragile time between night and morning, in the lot between the Baptist church and the trailer park where the father lies in the blackness of drunken, dreamless slumber, while the mother watches television in a state further west.
Through stations of isolation and regret.

She walks.
Through the blossoming gray of a lava field.
Through the masters' solicitations to buy and sell.

The quavering of a bowstring released.

Genuflection before fallen bodies.
Glowing in craters.

Before the crashing of a surfer spangled wave.
Diagonally through the persimmon trees.
Across vernacular lobes of sky.

Through flashing snow.
Catacombs.
And heaven descending.

The figure follows her.
Like a thing which is either projected from her body, or which projects her body from its own.
It follows her to the door of Beaver's house.

And, as she raises her hand to knock on the door, the figure raises one of its own and taps her on the shoulder.
Catfish whirls around and her eyes widen.
"Mink!" she shouts. "What on earth are you doing here?"

"This is my house, Catfish.
"You've been sleeping on the couch for a couple days now.
"We've been tip-toeing around, trying not to disturb you, but today, when I came in from the garden, you were gone, so I went looking for you, for hours on the paths, until finally I saw you, ahead of me, walking back to the house.

"Are you feeling better now?"
"I don't know. I feel like I've lost something.

"Where's Fox?"
"In town, on business."
"Have you separated?"

"No. We're drawn to one another too strongly for that. We just fight a lot.

"Because we have the nasty habit of becoming what we desire, he keeps turning into me and I keep turning into him, back and forth.

"And each time, in this little orbit of ours, when we pass into each other's places, we glance off of one another in a little celestial collision. I suppose we'll hit head-on some day.

"That will either be a very good day or a very bad day."
"Depending on how willing you are to let go of yourselves?"
"Yes, and I'm afraid we've got a lot of work to do, Fox and I."

"Are you feeling better," Mink asks again.
"I'm still not sure," says Catfish.
"Well, I'm certainly relieved to see you up and speaking coherently.

"I'm really sorry about what happened the other night."
"The other night," Catfish murmurs. "I can hardly remember."
"It's probably better that way... I mean, what we said wasn't important."

"It's getting chilly," says Mink. "Would you like to come inside?"
"Can I use your phone? I need to call Muskrat."

"Muskrat?"
"Yes."
"Who's Muskrat?"

"You know him. He's been here before."
Mink squints at her.

"Maybe you should come inside and lie down. I can make you some tea if you'd like, or soup. You haven't eaten in a while. You must be terribly hungry."

"I can't eat right now. I need to find Muskrat."
"Why?"

"I need to talk to him, to apologize."
"Come in and use the phone. Come in."

Catfish doesn't move.
She frowns and puts a hand to her forehead.
"What is it," asks Mink.

"I can't remember his number. I can't even remember where he lives."
Catfish starts to cry.

"Oh honey, it's alright." Mink holds Catfish. "I'm so sorry about what happened."

They stand in one another's arms, in the driveway before Mink's house.
The sun has begun to set.
The whippoorwill to sing.

Catfish finally pushes away from Mink and wipes the tears from her cheeks.
"I have to go," she says.
"Where?"

"I don't know."
"I don't think I can let you leave in your state."

"I'm fine. I'm just… just distraught. I need to think. I need a quiet place to be alone." Catfish thinks while Mink patiently watches her.

"My sister's cabin," she says at last, "that's where I'll go."
"You remember where it is?"
"Yes."

"Are you sure you're alright?"
"Yes."
"You remember my number, in case you need help?"

"Yes. Thank you," says Catfish. "Thank you for this."

Catfish grabs her duffle bag from the house, embraces Mink in the hallway, and says, "Goodbye… I think it's coming back to me."
She jumps in her car, guns the engine, and is gone before Mink has time to decide if she should really let Catfish go.
Mink stands in the doorway, watching a road so quiet you'd never know Catfish had been there.

As soon as she gets on the road, Catfish starts feeling funny.
Like the world's getting furry around the edges.
Around the frame of the rearview mirror.

The world seems to be wearing fur pants and a fur shirt and furry little slippers.
The wind picks up, cold and stark, and whistles around the car.
It whistles and it sings, "We are the children of all who died before us."

"Furry around the edges, that's all," Catfish says. "I'll leave the past at the door. I'll enter the purity of thought alone.

"The space that is itself all of eternity, all of space, all of mortality, of pleasure, of abject suffering, all the promised land of idea.

"Thought itself, and not the conclusion of thought, is the afterlife and the antelife and the life of life itself.

"Time out," Catfish shouts!

She pulls into the driveway of her sister's cabin.

No one's there.

She gets the key out of the watering can in the shed and lets herself in.

She goes straight to the bathroom, splashes water on her face, and looks in the mirror.

A muskrat looks back.

She vomits in the sink.

She's shaking.

She looks up again.

It's still there, where she used to be.

She screams and puts her hands to her face.

Muskrat screams and paws its face.

It's terrified of her.

She feels sudden, overwhelming pity for it.

"If you don't want me," it says, "then what were you looking for? Did you all have a different idea of what Muskrat was?

"Was it only a vessel to carry you?

"Was it only a moment, a vibration of spacetime, that you gave a name?

"Did the sound of a gunshot hang ponderously in the air, waiting for someone to decide?"

Muskrat rinses the puke from her fur.

She dries her eyes.

She hears a canary singing behind the mirror, a lamb bleating, a snake whispering something like, "Come a little closer…"

She places her hands on the sides of the sink and leans forward into the mirror.

It's dark at first.

Then a tiny, distant point of light grows until it engulfs her.

She's in a murky liquid medium.

A single atomic vessel of matter spinning before her eyes.

Then innumerable others swarming into view, passing the first in every direction without touching.

Then one draws near the first and they unite.

A third joins them.

A fourth.

And soon they are a seemingly singular hanging in the haze again.

Until another emerges from improbability and they too unite.

And they are together, of all myriad of forms spinning about them, a golden chain.

And then a growing forever outward through what she now sees is an inevitable ecstasy of attraction unto order until it is too much and then an ecstasy of separation into parts that continue the ritual ad nauseum.

Into infinite divisions of order.

Into one hovering before her eyes now.

Adds another to itself not in whole but by first breaking it into constituent parts.

And reapplying the attraction of the parts.

To summon motion.

Toward greater motion.
And greater attraction.
And the inevitable ecstasy of will.

Before her swims a protozoan.
The world clouds with motion.
Now it's a planarian.

She blinks.
Now a catfish.
Now a muskrat.

An endless accumulation of experience crushed into common being.

Until it can build no more.

And explodes.

Now a ring of humans standing around a smoldering crater, looking in, some moaning, some sobbing, some more silent than silence itself.

One turns and walks toward the mirror and looks in.

It is she.

The world begins to spin.

She tightens her grip on the sides of the sink, but it only whirls her in wider circles.

She staggers sideways and falls backwards into the bathtub where she cracks her head against the porcelain and sleeps the deep sleep of pre-consciousness.

And.
And and.
And and and.

It grows thus.
Into tighter and tighter knots of being.
It grows light outside.

She rises from the tub.
She gently touches the back of her head and winces.
She hears a deep humming behind the cabin and shuffles through the common room to the sliding patio doors.

Muskrat has landed between the cabin and the lake.
The ship is much larger than she remembers, and, while she stares in disbelief, the ramp slowly lowers from the underside of the ship.
She slides the patio door open and steps into the yard.

Figures begin to descend from the ship.
She can't see them clearly until they reach the dim light of daybreak at the bottom of the ramp.
Then she recognizes them.

There's Otter and Monkey and Eel, followed by Adder and Lamb and Cottontail, playfully elbowing each other, and then Bullfrog and Elephant and Jackrabbit and Mountain Hare, waiving to the wilderness as they come into view, and Mink and Fox, arm in arm, and Catbird and a fine young man, holding hands, and, finally, Muskrat, who grins at her and takes a bow, like a magician stepping from behind his assistants.
They all line up at the bottom of the ramp, hold hands, and take a bow together.

She smiles and claps until her hands are sore.

Then she and Muskrat step toward one another and embrace.
They hold each other, eyes shut tight, until they can bear it no more.
When they open their eyes again, the others are gone.

He's smiling at her.
"Where have you been," she says.
"Crossing the River Lethe," he says.

"You're so full of shit," she says.
"Yeah," he says, "I love you too."
They fuck like animals.

And later, lying naked in the grass, he says he's disappointed that he never got a good grasp of man's hubris.
"Excuse me," says Beaver. "Did you just say 'man's hubris'?"
"No," says Beaver's crap, "I said 'mons pubis.'"

"You said, 'mons pubis.'"
"Yes."
"Mons pubis."

"Yes."
"Okay, whatever. So, where the heck did I go in your story? Why wasn't I on the ship at the end?"

"Because you're right here."
"Because I'm here."
"Yes."

"I'm sorry," says Beaver. "I'm trying really hard, but either you're talking shit, or I haven't understood a word you've said. If you're omniscient, why can't you just speak to me in my language?"

"I'm just the world that passed through you, speaking not the language of ending, but of passing."

"Well, I don't think I've been hearing you right."
"You don't understand what I want you to do?"
"No.

"But I really appreciate the effort you've made trying to explain yourself. Why don't we do this: Why don't you take a break for a while. Take some time to think it over, and get back to me when you've got the wording figured out."

His shit is silent.
"Are you okay," he says.
It doesn't respond.

"I'm sorry if I hurt your feelings," says Beaver.
No response.
He's about to touch it, when he stops, looks around, and stands up.

"Okay," he says, "I got it. Everything's perfectly normal. I'm going to just turn around and walk away now."

Beaver buries his shit and walks back to the lodge, to the singing and the mead and Pickle, who rubs against his leg when he enters the hearthlight.
He never hears god again.
Its voice becomes earth becomes matter becomes form becomes dimension becomes distance becomes space becomes emptiness becomes nothingness becomes somethingness becomes a canary sitting in a tree at the edge of a pool, in a wilderness in a universe in a room far from here, singing a love song to whomever might be listening.

"If we've waited this long, we can wait another lifetime," she sings.

And she turns and enters the cabin.

Out on the water a muskrat turns its head, is still for a moment, then dives from sight.

"That's enough," Beaver cries. "Let it pass!"

"Alright already," you say.

Good night, everyone.

The band stops.

The bar is silent.

Someone at the back begins to clap.

MEATYARD
&
MISSIONBELLS

An Idealist

Meatyard pumps iron all day in his unfurnished, tenth floor studio. He never leaves. There's a phone number scribbled on the wall above the phone. When he gets hungry he calls it, and someone delivers meat lover pizzas and orange juice. When he gets tired he sleeps on a bare mattress in the corner. In the other corner is a transistor radio. When he gets bored he listens to the radio. When he gets bored with the radio he changes the station, or he pumps more iron, or both. Sometimes he stands in silence and stares at the river. He was told someone would take care of the rent. He doesn't know who, doesn't care. All he cares about is when the phone will ring, and what the voice will want him to do.

The Birth of a Notion

The phone rings. Meatyard drops a fifty pound dumbbell to the floor and grabs the receiver.

"Uh huh," he croaks. "Where… Got it… Uh huh."

He hangs up. He's naked. He wipes himself down with a wet towel, then a dry towel, then he puts on a black sweatshirt, red shorts, and black running shoes, no socks or underwear.

"I am a juggernaut," he says to himself. "I will walk through anything that gets between me and my target. This is what I have trained for. Amen."

He walks through a pile of pizza boxes and empty orange juice cartons. He opens the door and looks for a way to get down. He hasn't seen the hallway in a long time. A door across the hall opens, and a skinny, sweaty man in a pink bathrobe appears.

"Excuse me," the man says, "but are you okay? I heard banging in your apartment."

Meatyard stares at him.

"I don't have a problem with that," says the man. "I'm just wondering if you're okay."

Meatyard turns his head. He spots the elevator at the end of the hall and walks toward it. The man retreats into his apartment, closes the door, and leans against it. He stifles a sob.

"What have I done to deserve this," he says, "what?"

In a Bad Way

When the elevator gets to the fifth floor it stops, and a skinny, sweaty man wearing a Hawaiian shirt and blue polyester slacks gets on. It's the apartment manager. As the doors close, the manager recognizes Meatyard.

"Hey, Meat baby," he says, "great to see you man. I haven't seen you in, like, a really long time. Where you been hidin' out?"

Meatyard stares at the elevator door.

"Look, Meat, we need to discuss your rent."

Meatyard continues staring at the door.

"I mean, you haven't paid it in, like, a really long time."

Meatyard stares.

"Look man, I don't mean to be a dick, but this isn't a homeless shelter. You gotta pay, like, something, soon. Do you have any cash on you now?"

"You're not my target," Meatyard says.

"What did you say," the manager says. "Meat, man, you're starting to freak me out. Just give me fifty bucks right now, and we'll forget about it till next month."

The elevator stops and the doors open. The manager is now standing in front of

Meatyard.

"You're standing between me and my target," Meatyard says.

"What did you say? Look man, you're going out, so I know you got some cash on

you."

Meatyard slams the manager against the side of the elevator and walks out of the building. The manager runs to the front door, clutching his shoulder with one hand and his cell phone with the other.

"Man, you're fucked, he screams. You're so fucked! And I mean in a bad way!"

The Curtain

As Meatyard is walking down the sidewalk, a cop car pulls up to the curb ahead of him, and two skinny, sweaty cops get out.

"Excuse me, sir," says one of the cops. "Is your name Meatyard Johnson?"

Meatyard doesn't answer. He keeps walking towards them.

"Sir, could you please stop and answer my question."

Meatyard doesn't stop.

"You are standing between me and my target," he says, and he parts the cops as if he were parting a curtain, and walks through them.

The cop then sitting on the hood of the cop car says to the cop then sitting on the sidewalk, "What the fuck did he say?"

And the cop on the ground says, "That fucker is huge."

And the cop on the hood of the car says, "Tazer time."

And the cop on the ground says, "I'll call for reinforcements."

Meatyard Bound

A pack of skinny, sweaty cops tazer Meatyard into submission and haul him to the correctional facility, where he now does endless pushups and situps in solitary confinement, waiting for the door to open. And someone still brings him pizza and orange juice. And he still doesn't know exactly who pays the rent. And they don't know how long to keep him, since they're not exactly sure to whom he's a threat.

Assume the Position

"Hey, Meathead," shouts a guard, "you've got a phone call! Assume the position!"

Meatyard kneels on the floor, hands behind his back. The guard enters and cuffs him.

"Up," says the guard.

They walk down an aisle of doors, bathed in a dim, submarine light, through a gate, down a more brightly lit hall, through another door, into a small room with a small, thick window high on the wall before him. A payphone is mounted on the wall to his right.

"You've got five minutes," says the guard. "When I come back, I want you on your knees. Got it?"

He unlocks the handcuffs and leaves the room, bolting the door behind him.

Meatyard picks up the receiver.

"I'm here," he says.

He stands in silence and listens to the voice coming through the line.

"I don't understand," he says.

He listens.

"I understand," he says.

He hangs up.

He kneels on the floor, puts his hands behind his back, and looks up through the window. An airplane descends against a backdrop of clouds that look like the sand at the bottom of a sea. He imagines a body drifting in the slow, deep currents there. His arms fall to his sides.

"It's full of people," he mumbles, "alive and arriving somewhere."

He's in a city, but he can't remember which one.

"Hey, Meathead," the guard shouts. "Times up! Assume the position!"

Meatyard Breathing

Meatyard stops exercising. He sits on the edge of his cot and stares at the wall.

After the guard collects his untouched food tray, the guard lingers, peering in through the hatch.

"Something eating you, Meathead?"

Meatyard doesn't answer.

"What are you thinking about?"

"Nothing," says Meatyard.

"Must be quite some nothing."

"Nothing and everything that fills it."

"Sounds real deep, Meathead. I hope you're not trying to tell me we need to put a suicide watch on you."

"No," says Meatyard. "Anything is better than nothing."

"That's good, Meathead, because we don't get overtime for suicide watch."

"My name is Meatyard."

"That's good. Keep thinking like that, Meathead. Maybe you'll learn something." The guard shuts the hatch and leaves.

Meatyard closes his eyes, takes a deep breath, and holds it until he can't hold it anymore.

Now Eat

The hatch slides open, and the guard slides in a tray of food.

"Your favorite," he says. "Pizza."

Meatyard grunts.

The guard stands there, staring at Meatyard through the hatch. He's still sitting on the edge of his cot.

"What's it this time," says the guard.

"Time," says Meatyard.

"What about it?"

"There must be a difference between time and eternity."

"Why's that?"

"Time is infinite Nows. Eternity is a single Now."

"What about history?"

"History," Meatyard says.

"That's right, history."

Meatyard is quiet.

"I'm waiting," says the guard.

"Well, history is a perpetual creation of each living being. No two histories are alike, yet all are always and only Now. They are the experience of being in time."

"Well," says the guard, "it's about time you started talking sense. Now eat, will you."

Confidentiality

"Good news, Meathead," says the guard through his hatch. "Due to the recession and the decreasing value of government bonds, our budget's been slashed. We have to release twenty percent of our inmates. What do you think of that?"

"You could turn the heat down, feed us less, and reduce the requisite number of guards by never letting us out of our cells."

The guard's eyes narrow.

"Now, Meathead," he says, "that would be downright inhumane. As much as I hate my job, I wouldn't want to lose it. You weren't in corporate management before you fell into our lap, were you, Meathead?"

"No. Not really."

"Not really?"

"No."

"You don't think so?"

"No."

"No, you think so, or yes, you don't think so?"

"No, I don't think so."

"Are you listening to me?"

"I'm listening."

The hatch closes. The door opens and the guard enters Meatyard's cell and closes the door behind him. He stands before the door, his left hand resting on his baton, and his right hand resting on his holster. Meatyard rises from his cot and stands facing the guard.

"I like you, Meathead," says the guard, "which means that after you've left here, I don't ever want to see you again. But you're going to have to help me in order for that to happen. I need more than yeses and nos. Is that clear?"

"Why should I leave," says Meatyard.

"Much better," says the guard. "You should leave because the world is waiting for you out there. I'm sure you've got business to attend to."

"My world is the same wherever I am."

"Okay, let me rephrase that. You should leave because I want you to, and because you've got no better reason to stay besides some kind of existential apathy. I don't have that problem, so you'll do what I want, when I want it. And the first thing you'll do is answer my questions. Number one: why are you here?"

"Resisting arrest."

"Why did you resist arrest?"

"Refusal to comply with verbal orders."

"Why did you refuse to comply with verbal orders?"

"Refusal to answer questions."

"Why did you refuse to answer questions?"

"I swore an oath."

"What oath?"

"Not to divulge information."

"What information?"

"Where I was going."

"Where were you going?"

"An apartment."

"What for?"

"Business."

"What kind of business?"

"Human resource management."

"You told me you weren't involved in management. Did you lie to me?"

"I said I wasn't sure."

"How can you not be sure?"

"I delivered bad news."

"Bad news. You mean you fire people?"

"In a sense."

"In a sense?"

"Yes."

"You deliver bad news."

"Delivered. I've been relieved."

"You've been fired."

"Yes."

"What kind of company did you work for?"

"A consultancy subcontractor."

"Which one?"

"I can't say."

"Why not?"

"Confidentiality clause in my contract."

"Confidentiality clause?"

"Confidentiality clause."

"Confidentiality."

"Yes."

Promise

The next morning, the guard throws Meatyard's cell door open and stands in the doorway.

"Congratulations, Meathead! You're a free man! Now start walking."

They walk down the hall, through a door, past the phone room, past a guard station, down a hall, through a gate, past a number of empty cells, past another guard station, through another gate, down another hall, to a window where a fat man hands Meatyard his shorts, sweatshirt, and sneakers, and points him to another door.

"Change in there," the man says.

Meatyard looks down at the clothing in his hands.

"Can I keep my uniform on," he asks.

The man looks at him, then at the guard, who shrugs his shoulders.

"No, you certainly cannot," says the man. "It's state property. Change in there."

Meatyard enters the changing room and closes the door.

"What's wrong with him," says the man to the guard.

"Seems like he doesn't want to wear his old clothes."

"Whatever," says the man. "Should have thought of that when he put them on the first time."

The door opens and Meatyard steps out in his old work clothes. They're loose on him now. He hands his orange jumpsuit to the fat man.

"This way," says the guard.

They walk down another hallway, through another gate, down another hallway, and through a door into the blinding sunlight of early summer.

"It's been a pleasure knowing you, Meatyard," says the guard.

Meatyard looks at him and blinks.

The guard holds out his hand.

"Promise I'll never see you again," the guard says.

Meatyard takes his hand and nods.

"Now and forever," says the guard.

He lets go of Meatyard's hand and steps back through the doorway, into Meatyard's past.

Meatyard turns to face the city.

"Forever," he says.

Get On

Before Meatyard lie miles of brownfield and warehouses, stretching to the horizon, where they rise into a grey scar of skyline. The sky itself is oppressively clear and bright. He's standing in the correctional facility parking lot, hand shielding his eyes from the sun. Several men stand listlessly at a bus stop near the edge of the lot. He joins them.

They stand in silence for several minutes. Then a curly-haired, young man turns to the bald man beside him and says, "So, what are you out for?"

"Pacifism," says the man.

"Pacifism?"

"I hate violence," he says. "But no one believed me. They kept pushing me. Finally they got what they wanted. I beat one of them real good. Now they're happy. And I'm ashamed as hell. No one will ever believe me again."

"Does it matter if they believe you?"

The man doesn't answer.

"Well, I believe you," says the young man. "And I know that sometimes you have to fight for your beliefs."

The other men nod their heads.

"What about you," the young man says to a man in a trench coat. "What are you out for?"

"Statuary rape," he says.

The other men glance at him.

"Umm," says the young man, "how old was she?"

"One hundred and forty two years," the man says.

"Good god," says the young man. "How could that possibly be statutory rape?"

"She's a statue," the man says, "in Freedom Park."

He looks wistful for a moment and adds, "I love her little nubs."

"Indecent exposure," says the pacifist.

The young man turns toward a thin, grey-haired man in coveralls, and asks him what he's out for.

"Out of what," the man asks.

"What are you out of prison for?"

"I was in prison?"

The exhibitionist interrupts. "That's Jimson," he says. "He can't remember anything for longer than half an hour. He got gang raped and beat nearly to death in the laundry room because Chicory liked him but he was rejecting Chicory's offers. He's got brain damage now."

"I was raped?"

"Don't worry," says the pacifist. "You'll forget about it."

"I was raped? What do I do now?"

"Jesus, why'd you have to tell him?"

"This young gentleman wanted to know."

They all stand in silence. Jimson stares at the ground, mumbling to himself, nervously rubbing his boot over something on the pavement.

"I'm afraid to ask," says the young man, looking at Meatyard now, "but you're the last one, and I'd hate to leave you out. What are you out for?"

"Disorderly conduct," says Meatyard.

"Thank god."

"What about you," the pacifist asks the young man.

"That's right," he says. "I'm the last one." He stares at the skyline. "They were holding me for questioning, regarding the disappearance of my fiancée."

"Have they found her," asks Meatyard.

"No."

"Do you have any idea where she might be?"

"I wish to God I did," says the young man.

"Sorry to hear that."

"She probably just ran away," says the exhibitionist, "with another man."

"What's wrong with you," says the pacifist. "Don't say stuff like that."

"Sorry," says the exhibitionist. "I have a hard time keeping things to myself."

"Here comes the ten," says Jimson.

They all turn and look. The bus is still several blocks away.

"You can see that from here?"

"Yes."

They watch it approach.

"Well I'll be," says the pacifist. "It is the ten."

"My bus," says the exhibitionist.

"Mine too," says the pacifist.

It stops before the five men.

"Peace," says the pacifist, and boards the bus.

"Hello, freedom," says the exhibitionist, and flashes them before turning and boarding the bus.

The door closes behind them, and the bus crawls to the end of the block and turns out of sight.

The young man is still shaking his head. "He's not going to last long out here," he says.

"No," says Meatyard.

"He's got a big dick," says Jimson.

The young man stops shaking his head and asks, "Which buses are you two waiting for?"

"I can't remember," says Jimson.

"Where are you headed," asks Meatyard.

"I'm going to our old apartment. I figure that's the best place to start."

"Start what?"

"Looking for my fiancée. The cops have been through the place already, but I need something, and I wouldn't be surprised if they missed it. I need to settle things with the landlord too. Where are you headed?"

"I can help."

The young man looks Meatyard in the eyes.

"What do you mean," he says.

"I can help you find her."

The young man narrows his eyes. "I don't mean to sound suspicious, but I'm totally broke. Why would you help me?"

"I'm starting over," says Meatyard. "I want to help people."

"Right. Starting over. I have no idea who you are, and you have no idea who I am."

"You're the first person I've met," says Meatyard, "in my new life."

"Here comes the five," says Jimson.

They watch it approach. When it stops, the young man says, "Okay, fine, I could use the help." As he's boarding the bus, he says, "My name is Missionbells."

"Meatyard," says Meatyard.

Jimson looks confused.

"Jimson," says Missionbells. "Get on."

The Dream

They disembark in a mixed income neighborhood on the
east side of town, several blocks from the Ornery Mayor sausage
factory, and they start walking north, Missionbells followed by
Meatyard followed by Jimson, who stares about wide-eyed, as if
he's never seen houses before. The houses are small, with smaller
yards, if yards at all, and every third or fourth building is a two-
story, brick apartment building. An occasional car swishes past. A
lawnmower hums somewhere in the neighborhood.

Missionbells turns and ascends the steps to one of the
apartment buildings. Meatyard pauses at the foot of the stairs and
watches Missionbells take a key ring out of his pocket, fumble
through the keys, and insert one into the front door. He tries
turning it, curses, jiggles it, and tries again.

"Damn," he says. "They changed the lock. Damn... I wonder..."

He descends the stairs and walks around the side of the
building. Jimson looks at Meatyard. They follow Missionbells.
They find him behind the building, standing on his tiptoes in the
grass, staring through a large window into the dim interior of a
lower level apartment.

"Shit," he says. "All our stuff's gone. Someone else has moved
in."

Just then the light turns on in the room and Missionbells falls
back to his heels. They all step backward, away from the window,
into the center of a small tenant parking lot.

A young woman enters the room

Missionbells inhales sharply.

She's wearing spandex shorts and a sweat darkened t-shirt.
Her hair is drawn back in a ponytail. A few loose strands clinging
to her face. She breathes deeply and glances absentmindedly out
the window. She doesn't seem to notice them loitering in the
parking lot. She leaves the room briefly and when she returns she's
wearing only snug athletic undergarments, and she's talking on a

phone. She hangs up and takes a long drink from a glass of water, then leans down out of view. The lurid illumination of a television suddenly fills the interior. She stands up, finishes the water, and sets the glass on a bookshelf. Then she starts to stretch in the glow of some far away place.

"She's pretty," says Jimson.

"Is that her," asks Meatyard.

Missionbells shakes his head.

"I'm sorry," says Meatyard.

A car pulls into the parking lot and honks at them. Missionbells doesn't move. The woman glances in their direction and almost seems to smile. Meatyard grabs Missionbells by the arm.

"Wake up," he says, "we have to move."

And they're off, around the side of the building and down the street, someone shouting something unintelligible in the distance behind them.

Hunger

They stop walking when they get to a park. They sit at a picnic table.

"Would anyone like a cigarette," asks Jimson.

"You smoke?" asks Missionbells.

"I don't know, but I found a pack of cigarettes one of my pockets."

"You can't remember how long you were in?"

"No."

"Ah hell, give me one. Do you have a lighter in one of those pockets?"

Jimson hands him a lighter.

Meatyard glances at the street periodically.

"These are really stale," says Missionbells. "You must have been in for a while. You sure you can't remember what you were in for?"

"No."

Missionbells takes a drag, holds it a while, and slowly exhales.

"Sometimes I wish I couldn't remember," he says. "Sometimes I wish there was just a black expanse right back to before I met her."

Meatyard turns from the street to watch Missionbells.

"Sometimes I wish I'd been dead for the past four years."

"I don't mind not knowing," says Jimson. "I like the moment just fine. Like right now. Everything is bright and colorful and warm and we're talking. The crabapples look like pink fire."

"And they'll be gone forever, in half an hour," says Meatyard.

"It's gone forever every second," says Missionbells. "Now and now and now."

"There's always a new one," says Jimson.

"But you can't re-live any of them, good or bad," says Meatyard.

"I don't relive them. I live them, constantly, good or bad."

"Don't you wish you could remember how me met?"

Jimson looks at the table.

"I didn't ask to be this way," he says.

"Are you sure?"

"No."

They're silent for a moment. Meatyard turns to the street again. A carpet cleaner van crawls by. Meatyard squints.

"Aren't you having one," Missionbells asks Jimson.

"No," he says. "There's no point in starting now."

The other two nod.

"She left for Feary that morning," says Missionbells. "She was doing research up there for the IRS. She couldn't give me details she said, but she'd be gone all weekend. I didn't really believe her. We hadn't been getting along that well those last several months."

"Why not," asks Meatyard.

"It was really stupid. She didn't want to take my name, and I wanted her to. It was important to me at the time. Names and words and such. She was starting to think it was indicative of fundamental flaws in me. I was starting to think the same of her. Now I couldn't give a shit less. If only she were here."

He takes a long drag on his cigarette and exhales.

"She kissed me though," he says. "She kissed me and told me that what I didn't know wouldn't hurt me. That was it. Then she was gone. It sounded to me like she was admitting an affair. I was angry. You know, I think I still am."

Meatyard clears his throat.

"It sounds like we should go to Feary," he says. "But first you should get more information on what she was doing there. Do you know any of her colleagues?"

"Moodly," says Missionbells. "I think he would talk to us. But first I need to call my landlord and find all our stuff."

"I'm hungry," says Jimson.

What the Hell

They find a payphone.

"Does anyone have change," Missionbells asks.

Jimson hands him some.

He dials.

"Bob," he says, "it's Missionbells. Where's all our stuff?"

He listens and nods.

"Thank you," he says. "I appreciate it."

He hangs up.

"It's in a storage lot over on Pennsylvania," he says.

"Let's go," says Meatyard.

The attendant at U-Stor-It tells them he can't let them in until they pay last month's rent for the unit.

"If you let me in, I'm sure I can find my checkbook or some cash in my stuff," says Missionbells.

"Sorry," says the attendant. "No can do. We take credit."

"I don't do credit," says Missionbells. "It's against my religion." He turns to the others. "Do either of you have money on you?"

Meatyard shakes his head, and Jimson digs in his pockets and produces $3.75.

"Jesus," says the attendant.

"I know where we can get some," says Meatyard.

They take the bus across town.

"I'm hungry," says Jimson.

"We'll take care of that soon," says Meatyard.

They go to the post office and follow Meatyard to the end of a row of post office boxes. He squats down, produces a key from the waistband of his shorts, opens a box, and draws from it a thick brown envelope. He closes the box and asks Jimson to put the envelope in one of his pockets.

They stop at Taco Smell, eat a dozen tacos, and take the bus back across town.

Dusk is beginning to descend.

The attendant takes them down an alley between two long rows of corrugated metal doors. He stops before unit 14B and is leaning toward the padlock when he halts and says, "Damn!"

"What," says Meatyard.

"It's broken," he says.

"Open it," says Meatyard.

When the door rises, they are presented with what looks like a giant pile of trash.

Missionbells sighs.

"That's our stuff," he says, "dumped on top of my truck."

The attendant's eyes are open wide.

"It wasn't like that when we locked the door," he says.

"It's clearly been ransacked," says Meatyard.

"Should I call the cops," asks the attendant.

"No," says Meatyard. "We'll take care of it."

"Can we do it tomorrow," asks Jimson. "I'm tired."

"What the hell," says Missionbells.

That Night in a Motel 7 Somewhere on the East Side

"What do you want on your pizza," asks Missionbells.

"Anything but meat," says Meatyard.

"You don't eat meat?"

"Not anymore."

"And you," he asks Jimson.

"I don't know what I like. I'll try whatever you get."

So they dine on mushroom pizza and root beer, and take turns luxuriating in the privacy of the bathroom, shitting and sudsing up and standing under hot showers and beating off long and slow under no one's eyes but their own, the television filling the other room with the sounds of *Animal World*.

Then they fall asleep one by one. Jimson is the first one out, snoring gently on a cot in the corner. The room resonates with the sounds of a jaguar crushing a baby gazelle's throat. Missionbells turns the volume down.

"Where'd the money come from," he asks.

"Work," says Meatyard.

"What kind of work?"

"Confidential work."

"The kind of work that could complicate our search?"

"No."

"I'm determined to get to the bottom of this."

"I understand. I don't do that work anymore. The money is my severance package."

They're both staring at the ceiling now.

"I want to use it to help fill the emptiness."

"Doesn't everyone."

"That's not what I mean."

Jimson mumbles something.

Missionbells looks over at Meatyard. He mutes the television, and over the African savannah Jimson's voice floats.

"Who are you," he says. "Why are you watching me... Stay away... I loved her too much to do it... No... Comrade... No... Love..."

Good Morning America

In the dark before dawn, Jimson sits bolt upright and looks around wildly.

"What is it," whispers Meatyard.

"Where am I?"

"In a motel on the east side."

"Who are you?"

"My name is Meatyard. That man sleeping there is Missionbells. You and I are helping him look for someone he lost."

"Oh."

He looks down at his hands, then up again at Meatyard.

"Your name is Jimson," says Meatyard.

"Thank you."

"You're welcome."

"Tell me… can you tell me… how I got here?"

"We were all released from prison at the same time. That's all I know about you."

"Prison?"

"Yes. We don't know why you were there. And we don't care."

"Oh."

"You'll be fine. Go back to sleep."

"I'd rather stay awake now."

"I understand."

Every morning is the same.

Belonging

After a quick bite at Donny's Diner they're back at U-Stor-It, staring into Missionbells' unit.

"You've got a lot of books," says Jimson.

"I was an English major in college."

"What were you doing before your incarceration," asks Meatyard.

"I was detained."

"Before your detention."

"I'm an elementary school teacher. They had to bring in a substitute to finish the year. I wonder how my students took it all."

He starts picking his way along the wall of the unit.

"I need to find something," he says. "If you guys want to help, see if you can get the truck started."

"Truck," says Meatyard.

"It's small," says Missionbells, "Under the furniture and shit. An Iota."

"The tires are punctured," says Jimson, tracing its outline in the wreckage. His hand gets snagged in a pair of pink bikini underwear, and he tosses it aside.

"Could you put those in a box, please," says Missionbells. "Here, use this one."

"The break cables may have been cut too," says Meatyard, "and possibly sugar poured in the tank."

"Jesus," says Missionbells. "Can we do anything about that?"

"I think I can fix it," says Jimson.

The other two look at him.

"I think maybe I used to be a mechanic of some kind," he says. "But I'm going to need help getting it out into the light."

So Meatyard and Jimson set about extricating the small yellow truck from the heap of belongings under which it lies, while Missionbells searches for something he won't disclose to the others.

"Wow," says Missionbells, "I'm surprised they didn't confiscate this."

He holds up a lozenge tin.

"Does anyone want to smoke a joint?"

"A what," asks Jimson.

"I don't smoke," says Meatyard.

"Suit yourselves," he says, lighting up and bending back to an archeology of his former life.

Closer

Meatyard has manually hoisted the Iota onto cinder blocks, one tire at a time, and now stands beside Jimson, who's leaning under the hood, splicing together starter cables with a box cutter and electrical tape.

Missionbells is carrying belongings outside, sorting and repackaging them, and stacking the packed boxes. He pauses on the other side of Jimson.

"Do you know what you're doing," he asks.

"I believe so," says Jimson.

They all stand in silence a moment longer, while Jimson works. Then Missionbells speaks again. "Have you left someone behind?"

Meatyard looks up at Missionbells, who's looking at Jimson.

"Jimson," he says.

Jimson pauses, the roll of black tape suspended like an empty thought over the engine block. He straightens up, then leans backward, pressing his free hand into the small of his back.

"Ah, that feels good," he says. "You're asking if I left someone behind?"

"Yes."

"I don't know. Why do you ask?"

"You were talking in your sleep last night," says Meatyard.

"What did I say?"

"Nothing much," says Missionbells. "Something about love."

"Hmm," says Jimson, "That wouldn't be unusual, would it?"

"No," says Meatyard.

Missionbells raises an eyebrow and returns to work.

"I'm almost done," says Jimson.

"I haven't found it yet," says Missionbells, "but I'm probably getting closer… because I haven't found it yet."

Entre Acte

They take a break.

Meatyard orders pizza and has it delivered to the U-Stor-It office where they pick it up. They sit on the curb near a quiet intersection, Meatyard in the middle, with the pizza box on his lap, and they eat in silence.

Twenty people run past them, shouting, "On-on! On-on!"

When the shouting has faded down the street, Missionbells says, "What the hell was that?"

"Twenty people shouting," says Jimson.

"No shit, but what for?"

"They were probably members of an international running club called the Hash House Harriers," says Meatyard. "They were saying 'On-on' to indicate that they were still on the trail that the hare had set for them. Later they'll drink lots of beer and make jokes about the run."

Missionbells stares at him. "That's the most you've said since we met," he says.

"I used to run with them in Angola."

Now, four huskies run past on the transverse street. They are each attached by rope to a harness around the waist of a bearded man running behind them. The man wears a winter coat, stocking cap, shorts, and running shoes. The dogs run eagerly and silently. The man too. Soon they are gone from sight.

"That was neat," says Jimson.

"I'm going to assume that he was training his dog sled team," says Missionbells.

Meatyard, lost in thought, merely nods.

An aqua green van, with 'Carpet Master' painted in big red letters on the side, slowly cruises past. The driver is a skinny, sweaty man with long, greasy hair and aviator sunglasses. He doesn't look at them. He turns left at the next intersection and is gone.

"He's been following us since we visited your apartment," says Meatyard.

"Probably a cop."

"Maybe."

Eureka

"Ah hah," cries Missionbells. "I've found it!"

Jimson and Meatyard look up from the tire they're patching, just in time to see him inhale deeply of something in his hand and then slip it into his pocket.

"What is it," asks Meatyard.

"That, my dear Meatyard, is confidential."

They return to their work andMissionbells pats his pocket and mumbles to himself. "I won't let you get away from me this time." He resumes packing boxes.

The other two move on to the last tire. Meatyard rotates it into the right position and holds it still while Jimson inserts the end of a large syringe into the puncture and sprays a quick-hardening foam into the tire.

When they're done, Jimson plugs in the portable pump Meatyard bought, and starts filling the tires. Meatyard helps Missionbells stack boxes back in the unit. They all finish at precisely the same moment.

"Wow," says Jimson, "that was weird."

"I suppose I should call Moodly now," says Missionbells.

Meatyard hands him a cell phone. "I bought it at the hardware store," he says.

"Okay," says Missionbells. "Cool."

He dials and starts pacing back and forth in the alley.

"Hello," he says. "Can you connect me to Dick Moodly's desk? This is Nicholas Missionbells."

Meatyard commences hoisting each corner of the truck while Jimson removes the cinder blocks.

"Moodly. Hey, it's Missionbells… I'm doing okay… Yeah, it's been tough. That's what I'm calling about. I'd like to talk to you about it… no, nothing confidential, just, well, there's just so much I don't know. She never told me anything. And it's really getting to me… If I knew anything, even what it was like working with her.

Being a colleague… you know? It would make me feel better, like she was closer… Excellent. Where? Thank you Moodly. Thanks. I'll see you there."

He hangs up and looks up.

"Good work," says Meatyard. He's sitting in the flatbed of the truck. Jimson is sitting in the passenger seat. Missionbells reaches in through the passenger window and hands the phone to Jimson.

"Put that in one of your pockets," he says.

He turns and grabs a duffle bag from the storage unit floor, then pulls down the unit door and slaps on a new lock from the hardware store. He tosses the duffle bag in the flatbed with Meatyard. "Are you going to be comfortable back here," he asks.

"This is luxury to me."

Missionbells smiles, jumps in the driver's seat, and turns the ignition.

"Well I'll be," he says. "You boys did it."

Ahab's Coffee

People wearing calculatedly casual clothing sit at tables in the afternoon sun, sipping caffeinated beverages, reading newspapers, and tapping away at laptops. They're working hard at relaxing.

Missionbells pulls up to the curb and kills the engine. It backfires and everyone looks up. Meatyard hops out of the back, and the tiny truck rises a couple inches on its shocks. Jimson gets out. Missionbells is already out and approaching a bespectacled young man seated at a table on the periphery of the outdoor seating area.

"Moodly," says Missionbells, "I've never been happier to see you!"

"Who are your friends," asks the young man, readjusting his glasses.

"This strapping lad is Meatyard, and this fine fellow is Jimson. They're helping me out."

The man seated at the table nearest them gets up and leaves.

"Um… pleased to meet you gentlemen," says Moodly. "Please have a seat."

Meatyard grabs a couple chairs from the vacated table, and they all sit facing Moodly.

A barista appears.

"Can I get you anything," she asks.

"A gin martini, straight up, no olive, please," says Missionbells.

"I'm sorry, sir," she says. "We only serve coffee drinks here. And, of course, juice or soda."

"Right. I forgot. Bring me some coffee."

"What kind sir?"

"Just a coffee, please, black as hell."

"Of course. And you sir?"

"I don't know what I like," says Jimson. "What do you like?"

She smiles. "I'll bring you something you'll like. And you sir?"

"Water," says Meatyard.

"Carbonated, mineral, flavored?"

"Tap."

"Okay," she says. "I'll be right back with those orders." She disappears.

"So," says Moodly, "what do you want to know?"

"Why did Ana go to Feary?"

Moodly glances around at the other tables. Everyone seems to be ignoring them now.

"Well," he says quietly, "I can't go into details, but essentially she was evaluating the legitimacy of a mining corporation we were auditing. We suspect it's a pump and dump."

"Pump and dump?"

"A pink sheet scam."

"Pink sheet?"

"Penny stock."

"Penny stock?"

Moodly winces and massages his temples with his middle fingers.

"A company that doesn't really exist," says Meatyard.

"In a sense," says Moodly. "Thank you. It's a legal public entity, but it doesn't really do anything. It only exists so people can buy stock in it."

"Why?"

"So the people who started it can buy the stock at really low prices, build investor hype through internet spam, websites, etc, and then sell their stock when prices rise. Then they claim losses on the business they're not conducting, and pay no taxes. It's all profit, and we never used to pay attention to pink sheet… to small companies before. But now we are. It's a big problem. Are you okay? You look pale."

"She went up there to see if this mining company actually has a mine?"

"Basically."

"That sounds really bad, Moodly."

"It's a serious infraction."

"No. I mean why the hell didn't you send a professional?"

"She is a professional."

"No, I mean a detective or an inspector or something."

"Well, we probably will in the future."

"In the future."

"The investigation has been suspended."

"Suspended?"

"Until we figure out what happened."

"How can you figure out what happened without an investigation?"

"We're working on that. Influential parties are involved."

"Parties."

Moodly looks around nervously.

"I can't divulge details," he says.

"Oh God," says Missionbells, "this sounds really really bad."

The barista appears with their drinks.

"Here you go," she says, "and here's your special, sir. I hope you like it. It's my favorite."

She places what looks like a mound of whipped cream and caramel in front of Jimson.

"Wow," he says. "What do I do with it?"

Dreaming with Soldiers Two and Three

That night, they stay at a Super 9 Motel in the northern reaches of the city, where the suburbs start thinning out into fields of corn and wheat.

Missionbells, dissipated with drink, has passed out on a cot in the corner.

Jimson snores on the bed near the bathroom... out of which a gentle exhalation of steam still tumbles.

Meatyard double checks the locks, closes and latches the windows, sits at the head of the outer bed, back to the wall, and slowly slumps into sleep.

In the middle of the night, Jimson's snoring stops abruptly, and he mumbles in the darkness. "Hello... Who are you... Shouldn't talk to me like you have... I have a man... Paid to take care of me... Take the flowers outside... Away... Take us away..." The snoring resumes.

Just Familiar

They drive for hours, Jimson staring wide-eyed out his side window, Meatyard studying the road behind, and Missionbells the road ahead. The landscape gradually changes from a moist, heavy green to arid scrubland. The one commonality is the heat. The windows are open, the wind making their hair dance about their faces.

They stop at a gas station.

Missionbells mans the pump.

"Get some food," Meatyard says to Jimson, "and pay for it with the money I gave you."

"Money?"

"It's in an envelope in one of your pockets."

"Oh."

"I'm going to the restroom."

When he returns, the truck is parked beside the building, and Missionbells and Jimson are sitting at a picnic table, eating beef jerky and grape soda.

"Is that all you got?"

"I got some Flavoritos too."

He slides the bag toward Meatyard, but Meatyard shakes his head.

"Give me the money so I can buy some real food."

"I'm sorry."

"It's nothing."

When Meatyard's gone, Missionbells says, "He doesn't eat meat… I forgot, too."

"I'm trying," says Jimson.

"Like he said, it's no big deal. You'll start remembering eventually."

Meatyard returns with a bunch of bananas, several hard boiled eggs, and a carton of milk. He sets them on the table and sits beside Jimson.

"Help yourselves," he says.

"Thanks," says Missionbells. "How's the back seat treating you?"

"Fine."

"You're not getting sick?"

"No."

"You don't want to drive, or trade places with Jimson?"

"No."

They eat in silence for a couple minutes, before Missionbells speaks again. "I don't suppose you know anything about this town we're going to," he says.

"A little."

"Such as?"

"Well, it was a logging town, until all the trees were logged. Then they discovered iron, and it was a mining town, until all the iron was mined. Then it was pretty damn poor for a while. But that turned out to be a mixed blessing. Because they didn't have the money to modernize after the capitalists left, it eventually became a tourist attraction for people who want to see what a town used to look like before the modern era. I believe they've even turned the downtown into some kind of living museum, so it looks even older than it used to."

"Sounds like you do know something about it. Have you been there before?"

"It's essentially the same story for most towns up here. A typical third-world scenario."

"Sounds familiar," says Jimson.

"I suppose," says Missionbells.

Meatyard and Missionbells both look at Jimson.

"Did you say it sounds familiar," says Missionbells.

"Yes."

"You mean, as in you remember something?"

Jimson looks pensive for a moment. Then he smiles.

"Nope. Just familiar."

Enter Feary

The weatherbeaten sign at the edge of town reads "Welcome to Feary. Where history erases your cries."

"That's weird," says Jimson.

"I'll say," says Missionbells. "It sounds like a bad translation."

As the highway turns into Major Street, the asphalt abruptly ends, and the truck drops onto the dirt that composes all the streets in town. Meatyard grunts in the back, and Missionbells shifts into first. Grey clapboard buildings line streets from which a wind now raises skiffs of dust. The facades of the buildings are covered in gaudy shades of peeling paint. Before each building is a wood plank porch that approximately connects to the porches of the buildings on either side of it, forming a haphazard boardwalk of sorts. A leathery old man sitting on one of these porches turns his head slowly as they pass.

"Jesus," says Missionbells. "This place looks like the wild west or something."

"That old guy was holding a toilet plunger," says Jimson.

"Keep your eyes peeled for Leatherflower Boulevard," says Missionbells. "It's supposed to intersect this street."

"What's there?"

"The coroner's office."

"Why are we going there?"

Missionbells drives in silence a moment before answering. "Evidence," he says finally. "I've been told they have some evidence. I want to see it."

"Oh."

A man walking on the boardwalk stops and squints at them from under the shadow of a wide-brimmed hat. A glint of teeth. A pregnant dog limps across a side street named after some great man.

"Charming place," says Missionbells.

"There's your street."

The Coroner

They step from the blinding sunlight of the street into the twilight of a room lit only by a shaft of smoke slanting downward from a single small window to their left. The front room is empty but for a large wooden desk before them. Behind it sits a pale, mustachioed man, a tumbler of what appears to be whiskey before him, and an overflowing ashtray beside it. When the three of them have entered and stand uncertainly inside the doorway, he takes a long drag on his cigarette. Behind the light of the brightening ember, they see his eyes narrow at them.

"Can I help you," he says, exhaling.

"We're here to identify remains," says Missionbells.

"Is that so," says the man. "What's your name?"

"Nicholas Missionbells."

"Missionbells," says the man. "I've heard of you. Fiancé of the gal that went missing. And these men?"

"Meatyard and Jimson. They're friends."

"Friends."

"Yes."

"You want to see the evidence."

"Yes."

The man drains his tumbler.

"Are you sure?"

"No, I'm not sure. But it's all I can do."

The man rubs his chin.

"Alright," he says, "I'll take you back to the cooler, but those two will have to stay here."

Missionbells looks at the others. Meatyard shrugs.

"Okay," he says, "let's go."

Rememberment

The coroner leads Missionbells into a gas-lit, cedar-lined room, in the center of which lies a massive block of luminous blue ice with wood chips and cigarette butts piled up around it, and, around that, a dozen stainless steel tables supporting bodies in various stations of decay. Missionbells holds his nose.

"Good god," he says. "The odor. Don't you have refrigeration?"

The coroner grinds his cigarette out underfoot.

"You're standing in it," he says. "We're all-natural here. Anything else would be against code."

"For a small town, you've got a lot of bodies."

"Yup."

He leads Missionbells to the furthest table. In the center of it lies a toe. A pinky toe, garnished with red nail polish.

"Here it is," says the coroner.

"This is it?"

"That's it. Does it look familiar?"

Missionbells leans over and studies it, his lower lip firmly clenched between his teeth. The coroner rolls it over with his finger, and Missionbells flinches. His eyes take on a glassy sheen which he tries to blink back.

"I don't know," he says. "I should have looked at her toes more."

"Indeed," says the coroner. He lights another cigarette and says, "It's the right."

"I'm sorry… the what?"

"It's from the right foot."

Missionbells shakes his head.

"You tried a DNA match, didn't you?"

"Yes, but someone cleaned your apartment with exceptional care before the search warrant was granted." He narrows his eyes at Missionbells. "We couldn't find any satisfactory samples."

Missionbells stares at the toe.

The coroner drags deeply on his cigarette.

"How good are you at reconstruction," he asks Missionbells. "When you see a bit of flesh on a woman, how much can you imagine? How far can you go if, say, you're given an ankle, or, perhaps, an entire foot? Can you make it to the calf? The knee? The thigh? How high can your mind climb, Missionbells? I sit here for hours every day, trying to find my own limits. If she were alive, I'd be ashamed. But we both know that's unlikely, don't we? I sit here and make my calculations and try to imagine every part of her, try to uncover every inch of her forbidden frame. So I might know who this woman was. So I might stop her from dying in my mind… We can learn a lot from bodies, can't we Missionbells?"

Missionbells wipes his shirt sleeve across his face. The coroner takes another drag on his cigarette.

"Would this help," asks Missionbells. He draws a piece of white cloth from his pocket.

"What is it?"

"Her handkerchief."

The coroner's eyes widen.

"She used a handkerchief?"

"Yes. She always had one on her. She bought this monogrammed one for me, but I never used it, so she did. Whoever went through our apartment must have thought it was mine."

The coroner tosses his cigarette to the floor and holds out his hand.

"It's used?"

"Of course."

The coroner grins as Missionbells hands it to him.

"This could be our ticket, my boy."

He unfolds the handkerchief and holds it up to the light.

"Ah, yes," he says. "Nice spread pattern. A fine specimen. Good work. I'll get this to the lab pronto."

Missionbells looks down at the toe, then up at the coroner, who is admiring the handkerchief from different angles. "Where was the evidence found?"

"The old quarry."

"Do you know who may have seen Ana last?"

The coroner looks at him. "Ana?"

"My fiancée."

"Of course. Word is the guru was the last to see her."

"The guru?"

"He's a swami that lives in the ashram at the north end of Major Street. It's an adobe building. You can't miss it."

Halfcaulk

Jimson says he's hungry, so they walk to the diner across the street. Meatyard, hindmost of the three, pauses before entering. He turns and glances up the street.

Inside, he asks the others to order him a Shepard's Pie, no meat, and excuses himself to go to the restroom. He turns down the hall that leads to the restrooms and keeps going, past the restrooms, out the back door, into the alley, and then he's off at a sprint, up the alleyway. He follows it up two blocks, then glides up the side street, slipping between the wall of a feed store and the green carpet cleaner van parked just far enough forward that the driver can easily lean forward and glance down Leatherflower Boulevard. In one fluid motion, he wrenches open the passenger door, slides into the enclosed cab, twists the Glöck 9mm from the driver's rising right hand, ejects the clip onto the passenger side floor, and hands the gun back to the driver.

"Meatyard," the driver says.

"Halfcaulk," says Meatyard.

"It's been awhile."

"Not long enough."

The man runs his left hand through his hair and removes his sun glasses. A muted groan and rattle of chain seems to emanate from the sealed back of the van. Then a moment of silence.

"Well," says Halfcaulk, "are you planning to kill me?"

"No."

"Then what, may I ask, are you doing?"

"I'm letting you know that I'm watching you."

"What a coincidence. However, I must say that, to an impartial observer, it might appear as though you're doing a bit more than keeping an eye on me. Why exactly have you returned to this place? I didn't particularly like having to come here the first time."

"If you'd done your job right the first time," says Meatyard, "neither of us would be here now."

"The nature of my methodology isn't the subject of this conversation. I want to know why you've returned, with outsiders, who, unless your behavior changes, are soon to become liabilities."

"I'm not in the business anymore."

"How quaint. Come on, Meatyard. You know that's not possible. Everyone's in the business. There's nothing outside the business. You're either dead or you're getting there, on your own or with help."

"The meaning of his life now is to find out what happened to her, and I'm determined to help him define his life."

"Have you completely fucking lost it? I don't know the details of how you recently got yourself incarcerated, but I'm sure this new plan of yours is even more fucking brilliant. You think my methods are unsound? Step back and look at yourself. Did they fuck your brains out in prison? You're going to expose us, like some fucking underworld tour guide. Is that it? Do you fancy yourself a ferryman now?"

"You could look at it that way."

"Well it better not come to that, because, unless you kill me right now, I'll be ready and waiting for all of you if that happens."

"Something to look forward to," says Meatyard. "Just remember: he's mine."

And then he's gone, out the door and back down the alley, before Halfcaulk can reload.

When he gets back to the table, he's sweating. The food has arrived, and the others have begun to eat.

"Are you okay," asks Missionbells.

"Big turd?" asks Jimson.

"Yes."

My Head Is Starting to Hurt

When they enter the adobe structure, they find themselves in a small foyer. The interior is finished in white adobe as well. Benches line the walls. A young woman in loose white garments emerges from a back room and stands before them.

"Greetings," she says. "Our guest houses are full, but I would be happy to assist you in any other way… within reason…"

She pauses when her eyes pass over Jimson.

"Have you been here before," she asks. "You look familiar."

"I don't know," he says.

She raises an eyebrow.

"We're sorry to bother you," says Missionbells, "but we're actually here to speak with the guru. My fiancée went missing in this area a couple months ago, and I heard that the guru may have been the last person to see her. I'd like to ask him some questions, if that's possible."

"I see," she says. "I'll see if that's possible."

She disappears into the back.

Missionbells turns to Jimson.

"You look familiar to her," he says.

Jimson shrugs. "I wouldn't mind if she knew who I was," he says.

The young woman reappears.

"That was fast," says Missionbells.

"He can see you right now," she says. "But he only has half an hour before his meditation."

"That should be more than enough time."

She raises an eyebrow again.

"I should warn you," she says. "He's been a little cranky lately. He just emerged from thirty days of solitary contemplation in the darkness room. His meditations made him aware of previously unknown obstacles in his path to enlightenment."

"Is now a bad time?"

"Not at all. No time is a bad time."

She glances at Jimson, who nods in agreement.

"Just be patient," she says. "Follow me."

She leads them down a narrow hallway to a second, more spacious antechamber. She points to a mahogany double-door. "He's in there. Go on in."

Missionbells leads them through the double doors, and they find themselves facing a bald man in black robes, sitting lotus style in the center of a room lined, ceiling to floor, with crimson velvet draperies. Three black cushions lie on the floor before him.

"Sit," he says.

They sit.

Missionbells looks uncomfortable. "Were you expecting us," he asks.

"For a couple minutes," says the man. "My name is Rananda."

"My name is…"

Rananda holds up a hand.

"We'll get to your names later. First, what is your question?"

"Did you see my fiancée, Ana Ionescu, before she disappeared?"

"Perception and causality are funny things," says Rananda. "Permit me to share an analogy with you. Two cars collide head-on at a city intersection, and both parties are killed. In the process of determining who was at fault, the authorities collect all witnesses. There were four who saw the entire accident, each standing on a different corner of the intersection. None of the witnesses knew either of the parties. All four are as impartial as a witness can be. However, upon interview, each witness delivers a slightly different account of what happened. One says both cars swerved before impact, but unfortunately they both swerved in the same direction. Another says it appeared as if they were intending to hit one another. Another says clearly the sun was in one driver's eyes, and the other driver probably couldn't see the oncoming silver car against the faded concrete. And the last witness says it was clearly an act of God. None can agree, and forensics can supply nothing more conclusive than that two vehicles had a head-on collision. The families of the parties are given neither the satisfaction of a coherent narrative, nor the vindication of blame. They can only accept that something happened, and the more it is examined, the more confusing the story will become. History is an accident such as this."

"You're saying you don't know if you saw her," says Missionbells.

Rananda breathes deeply. "What I'm saying," he says, "is that utopia can only be achieved by individuals, for themselves. Otherwise it's merely coercion, which is the antithesis of utopia. Collective utopia is nothing other than dystopia."

Missionbells frowns.

"Listen," says Rananda. "You cannot truly find her unless you listen."

"I'm listening."

"What we commonly refer to as instinct is, in fact, merely an inward force resulting from the pressure of environments, past and present, upon the individual's center of being, which is the initial condition out of which emanates a self or will, the outward force. All sentient beings, and characterizations thereof, derive consciousness from the dynamic interplay of these two forces, toward and away from the original state of the universe."

"Like iron filings jumping to life in the aura of a magnet," says Meatyard.

"Exactly," says Rananda. "There's only one question we're all trying to answer, at every point on this pointless globe."

"What's that," asks Missionbells.

"What's the meaning of life."

"Of course."

"And we here, in this little town, two hours from anywhere, are doing as good a job answering it as any one else."

They sit in silence. The whole world seems silent for long moments. Then, suddenly, a siren breaks out somewhere in the distance and starts growing slowly towards them like the crest of an immense immaterial wave, as if the spirit of the distant cities is spreading audibly across the land, engulfing it. And then, just as it seems about to enter the room, it passes, and quickly dies away. It's silent again, but now a malign silence. A dog barks in the street.

Missionbells glances nervously at Meatyard and Jimson. Jimson looks relaxed. Meatyard's eyes are closed.

Rananda breaks the new silence. "What you're thinking now," he says, "could be the answer. But who's to know unless someone tells us when we've got it right?" He raises a small bell from the floor beside him and rings it.

The young woman enters.

"Sophia," he says, "please bring us some tea. The special tea."

She bows and leaves.

Something about the three of you reminds me of a story.

"What story," asks Missionbells.

"My story. When I was younger than you, I killed a man over a woman, and the village handed me over to the dead man's parents for punishment. They abused me at first, and I took it because I knew I deserved it. After a month or two, they stopped whipping me and let me out of the basement. They made me pick stones and repair fences on their farm. Soon they had me tending the crops and the livestock. When my father died, they allowed me to attend his funeral in the neighboring village, and I didn't run away. Eventually they let me eat with them. I was even permitted meat on occasion. This continued for some years."

Sophia returns with a teapot and cups on a tray. She pours them each a cup and places it on the floor before each of them. Then she leaves again. Rananda raises his cup to them, and they raise theirs. They drink.

"This tastes funny," says Jimson.

"It is funny," says Rananda.

Then he continues his story.

"One day, without warning, they told me to pack all my belongings. They took me on a two-day journey to the frame of an unfinished house at the edge of a small town. 'This was the house that our son was building,' the father said. 'Now you must finish it.' So I stayed there all summer, working on the house by myself, and when I was done I returned to their farm and was shocked to discover that my master and mistress had both perished that summer in a house fire. The village released me from my bondage and allowed me possession of several of the couple's goats, as was know to be their wish. I had nowhere to go, so I took the goats back to the house I'd finished building, and I've been there ever since."

"This is the house," says Missionbells.

"Yes. I've remodeled it a bit since then, and added some outbuildings."

"What happened to the goats," asks Jimson.

"I ate them."

"And the woman," asks Missionbells.

"She went far away, and I never saw her again."

"I'd like to remember that story," says Jimson.

"Indeed," says Rananda. "Now, it's time for your names."

"Mine is…"

Rananda raises his hand again.

"I'll tell you your names," he says, "your spiritual names."

"You," he says, pointing at Jimson, "are Nick."

He points at Missionbells. "You are Moe."

"And you," he says, nodding to Meatyard, "are Eddie."

Meatyard nods, Jimson smiles, and Missionbells looks like he just saw a monkey fucking a skunk.

"And now," says Rananda, "I will bless each of you in the name of Kali."

"You," he says to Missionbells, "will experience the true nature of history, in person.

"You," he says to Jimson, "will discover the secret of eternal youth."

"And you," he says to Meatyard, "will meet the one who dreams your existence. And, in the end, all of you will find what you ultimately seek. Now go," he says, "for I grow weary." He rings the tiny bell again.

"Thank you," says Meatyard.

Sophia appears and escorts them out to the street.

"I hope he was of assistance," she says.

"I have no idea," says Missionbells.

"It's often that way," she says. She smiles at them and disappears once more behind the ashram door.

"How the hell did he know our names," says Missionbells.

"My head is starting to hurt," says Jimson.

Reenactment

It's early afternoon outside. Hot and dry. A crowd of skinny, sweaty cowboys is arguing in the middle of the street.

"I didn't know they had cowboys up here," says Missionbells.

"This here is an historic reenactment," says an old man sitting in a rocking chair beside them.

"You mean there were cowboys up here?"

"There are now."

The cowboys are shouting at each other now.

"Where's the audience," asks Missionbells.

"You are," says the old man. "Smile!"

He produces a Polaroid camera from beside his rocking chair and snaps a picture of them. Meatyard flinches. When the machine spits out the image he hands it to Missionbells.

"Courtesy of the Town of Feary," he says.

"Thank you," says Missionbells.

He hands the photograph to Jimson.

"Do they do this often?"

"Every Friday. But not always this spirited. I think you're in for a treat."

One cowboy knocks the other's hat off his head. The other plants an uppercut on the first's chin, sending him sprawling into the dirt. Friends rush in to hold them apart, but the first draws his gun and fires from the dust. The second staggers backward and sits in the street, clutching his stomach. He looks confused.

"Realistic," says Meatyard.

"Sure is," says the old man. "This is the real thing."

Now cowboys are running in every direction, guns drawn and filling the afternoon with smoke and explosions. Several lie in the street now. More come running.

"I think they're bleeding," says Jimson.

"Very realistic," says Meatyard.

A cowboy is running toward them, looking backward and firing. His hat flies off and the wooden beam beside Jimsom splinters.

"Holy shit," shouts Missionbells. "They're using live rounds! Let's get the hell out of here!"

They try reentering the ashram, but the door is locked. Missionbells starts running toward his truck when the windshield shatters and the front left tire deflates with an angry hiss.

"My fucking truck! We just fixed it!"

"This way," shouts Meatyard.

They run up the boardwalk, duck into the first open door, slam it behind them, and throw the deadbolt. They turn and face the interior. A wooden desk, a couple chairs, and a full gun rack. The back of the room is barred off into a large holding cell with a single toilet standing awkwardly in the center of it.

"I can't believe what's going on here," says Missionbells. "I just can't."

"This is a jail," says Jimson. "Where are the police?"

A fresh crackle of gunfire erupts in the street, and the frosted front window blooms into a prismatic web.

"We need to find a back exit," says Meatyard. "Someone check the hallway, and someone look downstairs. I'll keep an eye on the front door."

The other two disappear.

"Nothing back here," shouts Missionbells.

"Down here," shouts Jimson. "I think I see an exit."

Meatyard and Missionbells barrel down the rickety stairs into the dark behind Jimson. At the far end of the basement, behind a subterranean jungle of pipes, light burns the outline of a door into the darkness.

They run for it. Missionbells hits his head on a pipe and curses.

"It's locked," says Jimson.

"It must lock from the inside," says Meatyard. "Let me look at it."

"God damn, my head is pounding," says Missionbells.

"You're right, it's locked, but not from this side. Strange. Stand back. I'm going to force it."

He plants his heals perpendicular to the door, turns his feet slightly toward it, crouches back and down, then flashes upward in an arc that ends with the tip of his elbow poised between a quivering doorknob and a splintered door frame.

They step into a blinding white room.

A naked white-haired man sits hand-cuffed to a chair in the middle of the room, a red ball-gag strapped in his toothless mouth. His pale flesh is filigreed with welts. A mustachioed police officer stands beside him, stripped to the waist. He holds a turkey baster in one hand and a bottle of Listerine in the other.

"Can I help you," he says.

Black Box

They stand in silence, taking in the scene.

Missionbells whispers to Meatyard, "The old man looks really familiar."

Meatyard nods.

The old man grunts and jerks his chin toward the officer, who dutifully reaches behind the man's head and undoes the fastening of the gag. The ball makes a moist suckling sound as he pulls it from the man's mouth. The officer then reaches over to a stainless steel table and picks up a glass with a pair of dentures soaking therein. He gently inserts the dripping implements into the old man's mouth. The man's jaw quivers, and he purses his lips as he positions the dentures, then clamps down and draws his lips back in a rictus, relaxes, and begins to speak.

"Good," he says. "You've finally arrived. Did you bring the box?"

The three visitors look at one another quizzically.

"I'm sorry," says Missionbells. "Do you know one of us?"

"Do I know you? I had a hand in creating you. I created the conditions under which you have come to this conclusion."

"This is not a conclusion," says Meatyard.

"Isn't it?"

"No."

"Truly, do none of you know who I am?"

"You look familiar," says Missionbells. "Are you…"

He pauses.

"Are you the president?"

The man grins.

"Do you want us to free you," asks Meatyard.

The officer tenses.

"No," says the old man. "I come here to find out what I know. No one else can know I'm here. If anyone finds out, you will be dealt with summarily."

"I understand."

"Now," he says, "bring me the box."

"What box," asks Missionbells.

"The one they found in Antarctica."

They look at one another again.

The old man motions to the officer, who crosses the floor to them.

"You," he says to Jimson. "Arms up. Spread your legs."

Meatyard tenses. Jimson assumes the position, and the officer pats him down, reaches into one of Jimson's pockets, and draws out a tiny black cube, the size of a pinky nail. The officer returns to the old man's side.

"Good," says the old man, "very good. Let's hear it."

The officer squeezes the cube between his palms. His face goes red with the effort. Then he exhales, leans down beside the old man, removes a hearing aid from the old man's ear, and gently inserts the cube in its place. The old man goes rigid, and his eyes roll back. He begins to speak in a deeper voice.

"...The nose of the dreadnought hits me from behind with such velocity that I am imbedded in it and voluntary movement is no longer possible. I cannot look to see, but I think my chest cavity has collapsed. My chronometer begins decelerating towards timelessness. I am silently and endlessly embraced by this titanic crush of radium alloy. Though my mind works faster than light, I am barely able to think. But I do. And though it may take me a millennium to make this calculation, I know that in one second of universal time I have traveled through the entire magnetosphere of the unnamed gas giant, and in the following second I and my mountain-sized cocoon of mad invention will plunge into an ocean of liquid metallic hydrogen. Everything but my indestructible black box will vanish between twenty thousand kelvins and sixty million atmospheres. Then all cognitive functions will cease. I will endure this momentary threshold for thousands of years. Whoever you are, who are able to retrieve my black box from the heart of this giant, know that when I was a man, faith in the evolution of humanity kept me aloft. When I became a god it was doubt that fueled me, doubt that made it possible for me to love them, doubt that allowed me to die for them. And if no one ever gets this message, then nothing will have changed. The red silence roars open before me. This is where I have always lived…

The old man stops speaking. His eyes flutter shut and his head slumps forward onto his chest. The officer leans down and carefully pries the cube loose with his thumb and forefinger. He replaces the hearing aid. Then he removes the dentures from the old man's mouth and inserts the ball gag again. He looks up at the visitors when he's done.

"You've done well," he says. "I'm going to ask you to leave now. I must revive him and resume the interrogation. The laws of the universe are contained in us as much as in anything else in creation. We need only ask the right questions and apply the right pressure. This man is the pinnacle of our law. If he doesn't know, no one does. Now, please leave."

They turn and stumble back across the basement. Missionbells bumps his head again on a pipe. He winces but says nothing. They trudge slowly up the stairs. Meatyard closes the basement door behind them and joins the others in the main room, where they stand before the front door, in the warm glow of light that oozes through the cracked, frosted window. It is deathly quiet.

"Wow," says Missionbells. "Wow."

"What was that thing in your pocket," Meatyard asks Jimson.

"I don't know. I didn't even know it was there."

"Of course not."

"Maybe there was something in the tea we drank," says Jimson.

"But we wouldn't all be seeing the same things," says Missionbells. "Would we? This isn't the way history is supposed to work."

"Maybe this isn't history," says Jimson.

"Maybe we're thoughts in the same mind," says Meatyard.

"Maybe these are the guru's blessings," says Jimson.

"Wait a minute," says Meatyard. "You remember that stuff?"

"Yes," says Jimson, "they're my earliest memories. First was the nature of history, then the man who dreams us into being…"

"And then?"

"The secret of youth… and then we get what we've got coming to us."

Entre Acte II

The baby finds it difficult to ride a pony. "Haven't these primates invented cars yet," it thinks. "Or motorcycles at least." It digs its pudgy digits into the pony's mane and starts yanking. The pony's eyes widen, and it starts to trot. The baby squeals with joy. Then it shits itself. Then it squeals again. The pony breaks into a nervous canter.

The Fountain of Youth

A baby rides down the street on the back of a pony, and suddenly the street is full of people. Women come running.

"Good lord," they cry, "get that poor baby off that pony. Who would do such a thing to a baby?"

A burly, bearded man staggers out of the saloon behind the infant equestrian whose pony is now nervously stepping in place at the center of a crowd.

"Oh no," says an old man seated on the porch beside our three tourists, "it's Black Frank, the meanest murderous rapist in town."

"There's more than one?"

"He never sleeps, and I'd say he ran the town… if he did anything more than drink in that saloon and kill someone once in a while."

"Is this a reenactment," asks Missionbells.

"Maybe," says the oldtimer. "I haven't always been here, so I wouldn't know. Maybe it's just an enactment."

Black Frank, swaying on his feet, surveys the crowd. When his eyes rest on the baby, an evil grin splits his face. He leans forward from the boardwalk and snatches the baby from the pony's back. The women all gasp and put hands over their mouths. Meatyard tenses.

One of the women shouts, "You cowards! Now Black Frank has him!"

"Well, well," slurs Black Frank, "let's see if it's a boy or a girl, so I know what I'm going to be fucking."

The women moan. The men grimace. Black Frank tears off the baby's diaper and frowns. The baby giggles.

Black Frank seems to sober up a bit.

"What the hell," he says.

He holds the baby closer and squints, his mouth hanging open.

"What the fuck," he says.

When he turns the baby around, to inspect the other side, it acts. The baby projectile defecates down his throat, and, after he drops it and falls retching to his hands and knees, the baby stands, puts its hands on either side of Black Frank's head and removes it with a quick twist. Black Frank's body twitches and blood geysers into the street. The baby turns the head over in its hands, considering the thing.

"That's a strong baby," says Jimson.

"That's a powerful ill-tempered little feller," says the oldtimer.

Missionbells is speechless.

A grinning man steps forward from the crowd and addresses the baby.

"I think you got it backward," he says. "Aren't you supposed to tear his head off and then shit down his throat?"

The baby sets the head down and stares at the man.

"Ha ha," says the baby. "You people make me sick. This isn't a show. Look how you live. Enslaved by some bankrupt notion of the past, worshipping what you fear the most, the sheer insignificance of your experience in the face of eternity. You think you control time through ceremony and sacrifice, but you're simply trapped in a bad idea. You will all die. Many of you will die hideous deaths in unimaginable pain. You can't care. You must clear your minds. Make them receptive. Make them as empty as you imagine your frontier to be. Reimagine your relationship with time. You are not colonizing it, you are it. You are time corporeal." He pauses.

"Now," he says, "someone bring me a tittie!"

The scene is interrupted by an eerie sound overhead, like massive windchimes in a breeze. Everyone looks up. A giant salmon is floating in the air above them. No one moves but the giant salmon which languorously arches its tail, as if righting itself in an unseen current.

"Mother," the baby pleads, "I don't want to go! I just got here!"

A soft voice resonates in the air. "You are too young my child," it says. "You are not ready to teach anyone yet. You have only begun your own education. You have not even begun your life yet."

"But I'm tired of waiting," the baby pleads.

"Do not despair. This will all stay with you as a dream."

The baby starts crying. A bright funnel of light descends from the salmon's belly and encompasses the baby. Then the light and the baby and the giant fish are gone.

"There's something funny about that little feller," says the oldtimer.

Missionbells is already at the door of the ashram.

"Let me out of here," he shouts. "Open the door and let me out!"

No Way to Escape

Sophia unlocks the door and follows them back into the waiting room. She is silent. Her eyes are red.

"We need to see Rananda again," says Missionbells.

She says nothing.

"Are you sad," asks Jimson.

"He's gone," she says.

"Do you know when he'll be back," asks Missionbells.

"I don't think he will ever be back."

"He left town?"

"He has awakened… transcended the material plane."

"Are you saying he's dead?"

"He was meditating in the room where you met with him. I heard him shout something, and when I entered the room he was gone."

"What did he shout," asks Meatyard.

"It sounded like 'where are the chitlins of thyme.'"

"We are the children of time?"

"No. Where are the chitlins of thyme."

"Oh."

"And then he was gone. I've looked everywhere."

"Do you mind if I look around," asks Meatyard.

She shrugs.

Meatyard disappears into the back. Sophia sits down heavily on a bench. Missionbells and Jimson sit on the bench opposite her.

"Was he not supposed to awaken," asks Jimson.

"He sought enlightenment," she says.

"Is it a bad thing?"

She shakes her head. "No."

"Then why are you sad?"

She stares at the floor.

"He didn't say goodbye," she says.

They sit in silence awhile. Then Jimson starts in again.

"He asked you for food?"

She shrugs. "Maybe."

"He spoke to you."

"Maybe."

"He thought of you."

"Maybe."

"Can he unsay anything that he said," asks Missionbells.

"Not unless he can erase it from our minds… from time itself."

"That's what I thought you'd say."

"Then he said goodbye," says Jimson. "He said something for someone other than himself to hear. It was the last thing he said, and it was the last thing you heard him say, you and only you."

"Maybe," she says. "Maybe."

"Have you noticed any other strange things that have happened around here lately," asks Missionbells. "Any talking babies or animals perhaps?"

She frowns at Missionbells.

"I've been preoccupied," she says.

"Of course."

Meatyard reenters the room.

"No signs of struggle," he says. "And no means of escape."

Soldier Four and the Girl

Dusk is descending when they say goodbye to Sophia. The street is empty again.

"Look at my truck," says Missionbells.

"I'm tired," says Jimson.

"We can walk where we need to for now," says Meatyard.

Missionbells grabs his duffle bag from the back of the truck, and they walk up the street to a bed and breakfast where they take a room with three singles. They climb the stairs to the room, and Jimson and Missionbells fall onto their beds and are asleep before Meatyard has finished locking the door and checking the windows. He sits on the edge of his own bed and waits.

Soon Jimson begins to talk. "I can't remember... Whose destination it is... Whose memory... Can understand life from inside it... Not a dream... I'm watching you... Your face... Wherever you go... Walking..." The last word ends in a snort, and Jimson rolls over into deeper sleep.

Meatyard runs his hand over the contours of his own face, then puts both hands behind his head and lies back, and for a time he joins them.

I Give You My Flesh

In the early morning, Meatyard rises and quietly leaves, locking the door behind him. He walks up the street to where it turns into blacktop at the edge of town. He does a hundred push-ups and a hundred sit-ups by the side of the road. Then he runs the ten mile periphery of town, keeping his eyes ever outward, first on the steppe, then on the glittering distance of the sea. He runs to the end of a promontory and stops. He is breathing heavily. He watches the rising sun burn on the blue eastern horizon. He thinks first about a beautiful woman he knew in Angola. Then about another woman he never truly saw, somewhere under the horizon now. He squats down, facing the sea, takes a pinch of dust from the ground, and places it on his tongue. He closes his mouth and swallows.

"I give you my flesh to carry you," he says.

Then he is off again, pounding against the earth.

Ablution

The others are still sleeping when he returns. He strips down
in the bathroom, fills the sink with cold water, and dunks his head
in it. Then he soaks a towel in the water and rubs himself down
with it. He scrubs his shorts and sweatshirt in the sink, then rings
them out and puts them on damp. He drains the sink.

Back in the bedroom, he sits on the chair facing the bed in
which Missionbells sleeps.

Time

Missionbells wakes up, scratches himself, and rolls over. He sees Meatyard sitting in the chair at the foot of his bed, watching him. He winces and rubs his temples and looks at Meatyard again.

"Are we still hallucinating?"

"Does it matter," says Meatyard. "Either way it's time."

"What's time?"

"Now is time."

"Time for what?"

"Now is when we go to where they found the evidence."

Missionbells raises himself on his elbows.

"I suppose it's time for that," he says. "I suppose it's time to go out there."

He swings his legs out of bed and sits on the edge, staring at the floor.

"It's always been about that, hasn't it," he says. "Now is no different than any other time. Not since she disappeared. It's all been leading to that quarry. I need to put on some clean clothes."

He walks across the room to his duffle bag, changes his clothes, and stands there.

"I'm not sure I'm ready," he says.

"It's time," says Meatyard.

Jimson yawns and opens his eyes. He rubs the back of his head.

"Where am I?"

"Feary," says Missionbells.

"Where's that?"

"It's where we are."

"What are we doing here?"

"Looking for Ana."

"Ana?"

"My fiancée."

"Oh."

"I'm Missionbells, and that's Meatyard. Your name is Jimson."

"Oh. Thank you. Pleased to meet you."

He sits on the edge of the bed and yawns again. "Do you want to go now," he asks.

"Yes," says Meatyard.

You're Almost There

They pay the bill and grab coffee and donuts on their way out the door. The sun is still low in the sky, but it's already hot. As they walk down the middle of the street, eating donuts and sipping coffee, faces peek out at them from second story windows. As they pass the truck, Missionbells throws his duffle bag in the back. They walk until they can see blue on the horizon, then they turn onto a gravel track that gradually slopes down into a vast clearing in the earth. They walk until they are in the middle of it, and there they stand and slowly turn to take in the entire excavation.

"This is owned by the company Ana was investigating," says Missionbells.

"Yes," says Meatyard.

"It's supposed to be some kind of mine?"

"Uranium," I believe.

"Uranium. It looks like an abandoned rock quarry."

"Yes."

"It's big. How are we supposed to figure out where they found the evidence?"

Meatyard starts walking. "Over here," he says.

Missionbells and Jimson look at each other, then at Meatyard. Light is beginning to waiver in the heat, so the farther Meatyard gets from them, the more he looks like a mirage, a vision drawing them onward.

"Let's go," says Missionbells.

And so they follow.

He leads them across the basin, to a spot near an indentation in the far wall of the quarry, and there he stops.

"Is this it," asks Missionbells.

"Yes."

Missionbells looks around, squats down and runs his hands across the stone and dust. He sits on his heels and stares at the ground for a while. Then he stands.

"I don't see anything. Are you sure this is where they found it?"

"Yes."

He looks Meatyard straight in the eye.

"How do you know?"

"This area was cleared. The ground has been swept."

Missionbells takes ten paces in the direction from which they came, squats, inspects the ground, stands and returns.

"Hmm," he says, "I think I see it too. Why would the cops do that?"

"They probably wouldn't."

"Hmm," says Missionbells, "I think I'm starting to feel sick again."

"Here's a tooth," says Jimson.

The others turn toward him. He's standing a good distance from them, beside the quarry wall, staring into his open palm.

Missionbells is immediately beside him. He plucks the tooth from Jimson's hand and holds it up to the light as if it were a diamond. He shakes his head.

"God, I don't know. It's an incisor. That's all I can tell."

Meatyard holds out his hand, and Missionbells gives it to him.

"Female," says Meatyard. "Mid twenties to mid thirties. Keep it."

He hands it back to Missionbells. The blood has drained from Missionbells' face.

"I think I'm going to throw up," he says. Then he does.

Meatyard leans down beside him and puts a hand on his shoulder.

"She's gone," says Missionbells. "I know it. I can feel it. She's gone forever."

"Probably," says Meatyard.

"Everyone is gone," says Jimson. "Except you two… and I only met you this morning."

"Forever isn't the worst place one could be," says Meatyard.

"I think that's where I am," says Jimson.

They help Missionbells to his feet. He wipes his forehead and his mouth on the front of his shirt. He breathes deeply and says, "What now?"

"There's a bunch of machinery up there," says Jimson, pointing to the far northern rim of the quarry.

"That's where we need to go next," says Meatyard, "where they used to crush the stone."

"Oh god," moans Missionbells, "why?"

"That's where the trail leads."

"What trail?"

"The one we're on."

"I don't know if I can take any more."

"You must. You're almost there."

The Hush of Dust

They climb a steep gravel track along the north wall of the quarry. The breeze has picked up, and when they emerge from the pit they find themselves in a pallor of blowing dust. A gravel mill looms before them, and beside it a Quonset hangar with a sliding door open to its dark interior.

"In there," says Meatyard, nodding at the hangar.

They enter the dusk of the hangar and stand still while their eyes adjust. Shapes begin to materialize around them. Several abandoned trucks, pulleys, lifts, fifty gallon drums, bins.

"This is it," asks Missionbells.

"At the back," says Meatyard.

Jimson proceeds, followed tentatively by Missionbells, then Meatyard, who scans carefully from side to side as he goes.

As they advance, the light recedes. The outline of a cement mixer floats into the murky field of their vision, then a chair, then the rear end of a van. Jimson stops walking.

"There's someone in here," he says.

"Jesus," mutters Missionbells.

He turns to Meatyard, but Meatyard is gone.

"Meatyard! Where the hell are you!"

The hangar door rattles shut, and they find themselves in a blackness broken only by an occasional shaft of dusty light seeping through a hole in the hangar's shell. Jimson and Missionbells stand completely still beside one another. All is silent but for the hush of dust blowing against the outside of the hangar.

"What the hell is going on," whispers Missionbells.

"I don't know," Jimson whispers back.

Then they hear it, the crunch of footsteps on gravel, approaching them from ahead.

"Is that you Meatyard?"

There's no answer. A leg passes indistinctly through a slanting shaft of light ahead. Then a moment of silence. Then the slow crunch of gravel again, growing closer.

Suddenly, overhead lights turn on, bathing the interior of the hangar in a weak sulfurous light. Before them, poised mid-step, stands a lanky man with long greasy hair, wearing heavily stained coveralls and night vision goggles. He has a machete gripped tightly in one hand.

"Fucking god damn Meatyard," the man shouts, "fucking up my plans again!" He rips off his goggles and tosses them and the machete to the ground. "Should have cut the power," he mumbles. He reaches behind his back and swings a sawed-off shotgun into view. "Looks like we'll just have to do this the old-fashioned way," he says. He nods to Jimson and Missionbells. "Naturally, you gentlemen know not to move a muscle."

Then he raises his voice. "Meatyard! I've got a ten gauge trained on Laurel and Hardy here! I know you don't think much of my 'inefficient' methods, but I enjoy giving folks a sporting chance, and killing them before killing you just wouldn't be very sporting! However! I do have other business to attend to, so if you don't show yourself by the time I count to zero, I'll start the executions without you! Ten!"

He turns his attention back to Jimson and Missionbells. "It's really unfortunate for you fellows that you got involved with Meatyard Johnson. Nine! He was trouble enough before he lost it, but now he's a downright hazard. Getting bystanders involved… very unprofessional. Eight!"

"Who killed Ana," blurts Missionbells.

"Ana? Sorry mate, I'm not acquainted with any Anas. Seven!"

"The woman who disappeared up here in spring."

"Ah, I see. You must be the heartbroken lover. My compliments. She was a tough little minx. Meatyard! Your charge here wants to know who deep-sixed his lovely! Do you want to break the news or would you like me to!"

No answer.

"Very well! With relish! Six! To answer your question, I started gently, with bribes, intimidation, and threats. Basic stuff. Phone calls, notes on the windshield, etc. It's strange she didn't confide in you. Well, she persisted in her stubborn idealism, so finally Fenris and I had to pay her a visit in the pit."

Missionbells takes a step toward Halfcaulk, and Halfcaulk discharges the shotgun into the ground at his feet. Missionbells falls to the floor, his boots riddled with tiny holes. Echoes of the blast reverberate in the air.

"Oh fuck, oh fuck," Missionbells moans. Blood begins to ooze from his boots.

"No need to hurry the inevitable," says Halfcaulk. "I like your spirit though. Like hers. It makes my job more rewarding. Five!" He steps toward an old office chair and puts a hand on the back of it. "After Fenris had immobilized her, I brought her up here for a more intimate setting, and I cuffed her to this chair. I apologize. I couldn't get all the stains out of it. Because of that I've had it in my van since then. I've reproduced it now for your viewing pleasure. You should feel honored. Four! In retrospect, I admit I probably should have ended her story sooner, down in the pit, for example, but her resilience intrigued me. She made it personal. Besides, I didn't have any other work that week. So we holed up in here, to see how long she'd last. Three! Like I said, she had spirit. She lasted until Meathead showed up. The agency sent him to take over because they felt I was becoming a 'liability.' Too involved." He raises his voice again. "A liability! Are you savoring the irony Meatyard! I sincerely hope so! Two!"

"Why," moans Missionbells.

"Because irony is all we've got," says Halfcaulk. "In this country. Without irony a man sweats in a ditch for twenty years, crawls out to give a woman some children, and crawls right back into his ditch to keep digging. When he gets too tired to go on, his sons crawl out of their own ditches just long enough to bury him where he falls. I decided long ago to have none of it... after I'd buried my own father that is. In the swamp. But that's a different story."

"Why did you kill her?"

"Oh, I see. Well, technically I didn't, although I was finding it difficult to keep her alive. Technically, it was Meatyard who got impatient and finished her off. One! Meatyard! Remind me! How did you do her in! What? No explanation? No description of how you squeezed the life from her with your bare hands? Pity! Well! You won't have to do it this time! Zero! Let's start with loverboy!"

Missionbells is on his knees, forehead pressed to the floor, arms over the back of his head, sides heaving with grief, when he does it. Halfcaulk lowers the shotgun to his head.

Jimson looks up into the air. Meatyard is falling silently there, his knees loosely raised, hands together over his head, as if in prayer.

"How did you do that," whispers Jimson.

Halfcaulk looks up, and the gun discharges into Jimson as Meatyard lands on Halfcaulk's shoulders. They all crumple to the ground simultaneously. Meatyard is the first up. He throws Halfcaulk's gun behind the cement mixer and runs to Jimson. He tears Jimson's coveralls open and stares down in astonishment.

"You're wearing a Kevlar vest," he says.

Jimson groans, "Is that what that is?"

"Thank god," says Meatyard and turns to Halfcaulk, who has crawled to the back of his van and hauled himself up to the door handle.

"I've brought us some company," says Halfcaulk. "I think you'll remember him."

And before Meatyard can cross the space between them, Halfcaulk opens the door, and a mound of slobbering mastiff ripples to the floor.

Meatyard stops in his tracks.

Halfcaulk strokes the dog's head.

"I see you remember Fenris," he says. "He's got quite an appetite. As I'm sure you recall, I couldn't keep him off her." He pats the dog's side. "Let's finish the job, Fenris. Attack!"

Meatyard plants his feet for the impact, and as the dog lands on him, jaws open wide, he drives his right fist down its throat and wraps his left arm around its neck. They both hit the ground, the dog pawing madly, gurgling, clamping down on Meatyard's arm, Meatyard wrapping his legs tightly around it's torso, working his fist deeper and deeper down the dog's throat, now clamping his other hand over its nostrils. Meatyard has worked his arm down its throat up to his bicep and now flexes it so tightly the dog's jowls look as if they will split. Its eyes are rolling, blood of man and beast foaming from its nostrils.

Halfcaulk whimpers and starts limping toward the cement mixer, but Missionbells catches his feet, trips him, and starts crawling up Halfcaulk's body. They wrestle, clawing at each other's faces for nearly a minute before Halfcaulk drives a knuckle into Missionbells' temple and Missionbells cries out and curls into a ball.

Then Halfcaulk alone sees Meatyard rise. Fenris slides limply from his arm, and Meatyard lurches forward, through the greasy electric glow, over the bodies of his companions, blood running down his arm. Halfcaulk starts scrambling madly, on hands and knees, towards the cement mixer, but, before it seems possible, Meatyard has flipped him over and has his hands around Halfcaulk's neck, with the adam's apple scissored between his thumbs. Meatyard begins to squeeze. Blood drips from his arm onto Halfcaulks'face. Halfcaulk shakes his head from side to side, growling deep in his throat, and claws at Meatyard's eyes. Meatyard looks up calmly, as if regarding something distant. Halfcaulk convulses, his eyes bulge, his face looks as if it will explode, and, suddenly, Meatyard releases him.

Halfcaulk gasps for breath while Meatyard sits calmly on his chest and says, "I can't do it. I made a promise."

Halfcaulk tries to crawl away, but Missionbells crawls up behind him and cracks him over the head with a pipe. They both fall back to the ground.

Now all but Meatyard are sprawled on the floor. All are breathing heavily or shallowly, but breathing.

"My stomach hurts," says Jimson.

"Why did you do it," asks Missionbells.

"It wasn't a job anymore," says Meatyard. "I decided when I saw what he'd done to her. She didn't fight me. She'd had enough. I did it for her. I told her that."

Missionbells is quiet a moment, then asks, "Where is she?"

Meatyard falls over sideways.

"Where is she?"

"The bottom of the sea," Meatyard mumbles.

Then all is quiet but for the sound of breathing and the dull hush of dust.

Zoia

A car door opens. With difficulty, Missionbells raises his head. A familiar woman steps out of one of the abandoned vehicles at the mouth of the hangar and walks toward them. She stops at Jimson.

"Good work," she says. "I'll get you to a doctor soon."

"Who are you," he asks.

But she's already walking again. She pauses over Fenris, who is starting to rouse. A gunshot echoes off the hangar walls, and he lays his head back down. She stands over Halfcaulk now. She rolls him over and cinches his wrists together with a nylon strap. He moans, and she punches him in the back of the head.

"Save it," she says. "You'll have plenty of time for moaning later."

She kneels down beside Meatyard, lays her fingers along his jawbone, is still for a moment, then nods her head. She stands and looks down at Missionbells.

"You," he says. "You're the woman I saw in my old apartment."

"Yes," she says. "I'm Officer Zoia. This is my case. I'm responsible for your release."

She grins. "And thanks to you boys, it's going to be a lot easier to bust those fuckers now."

The Secret Sharer

Nurse Jamestown goes about her rounds with a lighter step than usual this morning. When she arrived at the nursing station, everyone was talking about the three new patients the police brought in yesterday afternoon. The nursing staff were given little information about them. Only that they were brought it from Feary, and that they were to have separate rooms, that one had spread shot pellets dug out of his feet, one had them removed from his abdomen, and one has a hundred and forty two stitches in his right arm, presumably resulting from some kind of animal attack. One has amnesia. They all have saline drips and are on large doses of analgesics and antibiotics. No one is sure what exactly happened to them, but the nursing station consensus rules out a hunting accident. They're dying to know, but they aren't worried. They're good at this. They'll get the story from the patients themselves sooner or later.

The first is unconscious when she enters his room. He's a handsome, curly-haired young man. He could easily be her son. As she's injecting his medications into his I.V. he comes to.

"How are the others doing," he asks.

"I haven't seen them yet," she says, "but I'm told they're in stable condition."

He nods and seems to be deep in thought. Now doesn't seem the right time to ask, she thinks.

"Breakfast will be served soon," she says. "Can I get you anything else in the meantime?"

"No, thank you," he says.

The next one is awake and watching the door when she enters. His bed is adjusted so he's sitting upright. He watches her vigilantly while she works.

"How are they," he asks.

"Stable," she says. "How are you feeling?"

"My arm is stiff."

"To be expected," she says. "Would you like anything before I come back with your breakfast?"

"No."

She's about to leave when he asks, "Is the man with injured feet awake?"

"Yes," she says, "he's awake."

"Has he said anything to you?"

"He asked how you were doing."

He nods and looks pensive.

Isn't this some curious business, she thinks.

The next one is awake as well. He's looking nervously about him when she enters. She stops dead in her tracks and puts her hand over her mouth.

"Nicky," she whispers, then catches herself. "My god, is that you, Ron?"

"I don't know," he says. "Do I know you?"

She runs to him and throws her arms about him.

"Ronald, it's Anne," she cries, "Your old neighbor!" She holds him tightly, as if he's trying to get away, and says more gently, "Your old friend." He doesn't respond. After a moment, she pulls back and looks him in the eyes. "What are you doing up here?"

"I don't know."

Good Luck Gentlemen

Officer Zoia and the coroner visit them several days into their stay. They request a private meeting with all three patients, so Nurse Jamestown shows the patients to the break room where Zoia and the coroner are waiting. She brings Missionbells in a wheelchair. Then she leaves them, closing the door behind her. Nurses hover anxiously at the station down the hall.

"We got a positive match between the handkerchief and the toe," says the coroner. "That makes it pretty conclusive. Looks like we found her. More or less."

He lights a cigarette.

"This is a no-smoking facility," says Zoia. "Put it out."

He pinches the ember off in the sink and pockets the cigarette.

"Here's how it officially stands for each of you," continues Zoia. "Missionbells, you're no longer a suspect. You have our condolences for your loss. Meatyard, we've classified all charges relating you to this case. Since you've refused to testify, you'll not be eligible for the witness protection plan, but you can be assured that we'll be keeping an eye on you. We wish you luck in all lawful future pursuits. And finally, Mr. Ionescu, we welcome you back to your former identity. We hope your memory likewise returns and that you find it a solace rather than a burden. Until then, Nurse Jamestown has graciously offered to be your legal guardian. The hospital informs us that you can all be safely discharged in 48 hours. The state will cover all necessary medical expenses incurred up to that time. Are there any questions?"

They stare dumbly at her. The coroner taps his fingers on the counter, staring at the door.

"Well then," she says. "Good luck gentlemen. We appreciate the legal evidence that our surveillance of your activities has provided. We thank you for your persistence, and sincerely hope that no further misfortune befalls you."

She knocks twice on the break room table, salutes them, and leaves the room with the coroner in tow.

"Do you forgive me," asks Meatyard.

"Take me to where you left her," says Missionbells.

Antiphonal

After they've been discharged, Nurse Jamestown drives them down to the shore in her old Buick sedan. They get out and Meatyard leads them over dunes to the base of a rock outcrop where an overturned row boat lies half hidden in beach grass. They upright it, slide the oars in the oarlocks, and push it across the sand into the water. Meatyard and Missionbells jump in.

Nurse Jamestown takes Jimson's hand, and they walk to the top of a dune where they sit and watch Meatyard and Missionbells recede almost from sight on the flickering blue.

"You always had such good eyes," she says. "Can you see what they're doing?"

Jimson holds his hand up to shade his eyes.

Meatyard stops rowing.

"This is where I returned her," he says.

Missionbells leans over the edge of the boat and stares into the water.

"It looks deep," he says.

"About a thousand feet right here, with strong currents. Too deep for conventional recovery."

Still peering downward, Missionbells speaks. "She was an orphan. There's no one for me to tell this to. Here she is forever, in my heart alone."

"I will never forget."

"How can I be sitting here with you? What do I tell myself?"

"I've given it careful thought," says Meatyard, "and I've decided that, if you want me to, I'll dive down here and not turn back till I find her."

"They're talking," says Jimson. "Wait. One of them has jumped over the side of the boat... Now the other one has."

"What? In their condition? Fully clothed?"

"Yes. I can't see them anymore. They're both under water."

They sit in silence awhile, Jimson staring out to sea, Nurse Jamestown staring at him.

"Are they still under," she asks.

"Yes."

"Oh dear. I wish we knew how we ended up like this."

They sit in silence awhile longer. Jimson has started to chew his upper lip. Nurse Jamestown puts her hand on his back. Then, suddenly, a broad smile breaks across his face, and he stands up.

"They've surfaced," he says. "They've surfaced some distance from the boat, and they're swimming toward it... It looks like one of them is holding the other."

When Meatyard and Missionbells return, they are both soaking wet and shivering. They drag the boat ashore, and Missionbells falls to the sand, rolls onto his back, and lies there, panting. Meatyard sits on the gunwale, elbows on knees, breathing deeply. A number of his sutures are bleeding.

"What on earth are you doing," Nurse Jamestown demands. "You're supposed to be recovering!"

"We're alright now," says Meatyard.

"It is deep," says Missionbells. "It goes forever."

The Case of the Mysterious Sandwich

Nurse Jamestown takes them back to her house and throws their clothes in the wash while they take showers. Then she busies herself making sandwiches in the kitchen. Jimson sits beside her, drinking coffee and listening to her tell him about himself.

"I don't think I eat meat," he interrupts.

She looks startled.

"Since when don't you eat meat," she asks. "You used to come over to my apartment for pot roast all the time."

"I don't know. It just struck me now that you should make one of those without meat."

"Well I'll be," she says. "Maybe you changed, and maybe your memory's coming back."

Meatyard enters the kitchen. Like Jimson, he's wearing slacks and a dress shirt that used to belong to Nurse Jamestown's father.

"Well look at you," she says. "A little tight in the chest and butt, but I don't think the ladies will mind."

Meatyard smiles.

"Have a sandwich," she says.

"Do they have meat in them?"

She looks at Jimson. He's already half way through a bologna sandwich.

"Well I'll be," she says. "Here's a cheese sandwich I just made."

"Thank you," says Meatyard.

Missionbells enters, carrying his duffle bag and wearing a clean pair of his own clothes.

"A beautiful little place you have here, Anne," he says.

"Thank you."

She holds the sandwich plate out to him.

"Thank you."

He sits and starts eating.

"Coffee?"

"Yes, please." He accepts the offered cup. "So, I hear Jimson was a bit of a painter."

"Oh, yes," she says, "Ron was a renaissance man. In fact, I have some of his paintings in my shed. When he disappeared, he left a note asking me to watch after them. I'll show you when we're done here. Maybe they'll jog his memory!"

Goodbye and Hello

She brings them to a large garden shed with peeling white paint, and unlocks it. They follow her inside. Suddenly, unearthly landscapes surround them, hung from every available surface. Some stand on the floor, leaning against the walls. Light falling onto the floor from the western window casts them in ethereal footlight. The visitors stand in the center, surrounded by windows into other worlds.

"Amazing," says Missionbells.

"I painted these?" says Jimson.

"You sure did," she says. "I watched you work on one."

"I feel weird," says Jimson, "like I'm standing inside someone else's head."

"It'll come back to you," she says. "I'll help you to know who you were."

Meatyard stands silently before a canvas propped against the wall in the northeast corner. The others join him. It's a photo realist representation of a bald man in black robes, sitting lotus style in the center of a crimson room. The man is smiling at them. One hand rests on his thigh and the other is raised, as if to say goodbye or hello.

Soldier One's Dream

I couldn't breath... I looked over the edge... Saw dust and knew she was gone... Fell to my knees... Couldn't breathe... Can't breathe... Breathe...

Intentions

They stay at Nurse Jamestown's house for several days. Each day, while she's at work, they borrow her car and drive to Feary, where they work on Missionbells' truck. They eat breakfast and dinner together every day. When they've got the truck road-worthy again, Missionbells drives it back to Nurse Jamestown's place, and they have one last dinner together. When they are eating, she pauses over her own plate and watches her old neighbor, a wistful smile on her face.

When he looks up she asks, "Where on earth did you learn to fix automobiles?"

"Wasn't I a mechanic," he asks.

"A mechanic," she laughs. "Not the Ronald I knew. We've certainly got our work cut out for us, don't we." She turns to Missionbells. "So, what are your plans?"

"Well, I guess I'll visit my parents and go back to the city and find a new apartment and then go back to teaching in fall. I don't know what else to do."

She nods.

"And what are your plans, Meatyard?"

"I think I'd like to go back to Feary and stay at the ashram for a while," he says. "If Missionbells will give me a ride."

Missionbells nods.

"I'm going to miss you guys," says Jimson.

"I hope so," says Missionbells.

"Yes," says Meatyard. "I certainly hope so."

Nothing and Everything that Fills It

After breakfast the next day, they embrace and say goodbye, and Nurse Jamestown and Jimson watch the beat up little pickup chug to the end of the street and turn from sight. Then she puts an arm around him.

"Don't be sad," she says. "We'll visit them."

"Sure," he says.

She leads him back inside and shows him a handwritten note.

"I've got to go to work now," she says. "I'm going to pin this note to your shirt, so if you get confused you'll have it here to remind you where you are. It's also got my cell number on it, so you can call me if there's any kind of emergency. Does that make sense?"

"Yes."

"Good," she says. "Make yourself at home and I'll be back before you know I'm gone." She chuckles. "Sorry," she says. "There's a loaf of zucchini bread on the counter. It's your favorite."

"Zucchini bread?"

"Oh Ron," she says, "whatever happened to you."

She kisses him on the cheek and leaves.

He waives goodbye through the screen door and watches until she's gone. Then he turns and walks back into the kitchen. He's alone. It seems like he hasn't been alone for a long, long time. He finds a knife and cuts himself a slice of bread from the loaf on the counter. He takes a bite. "Mmm," he says. "This is good."

He walks into the living room, chewing. He stands before a bookshelf and inspects the photographs there. He doesn't recognize anyone… except for a woman who looks vaguely familiar.

"That's strange," he says. "I wonder who she is."

He wanders into the guestroom and stops before the mirror. There's a piece of paper pinned to his chest. He holds it up and reads it.

"Ahh," he says, "good to know."

He notices a paper bag on the bed. Inside he finds a pair of coveralls. He sits on the edge of the bed and pulls them out of the bag. They have lots of holes in them. And stiff, dark stains.

"There's something in this pocket," he says.

He reaches in and pulls out a half empty pack of cigarettes and a lighter. He reaches into another pocket and produces thirty five cents in nickels and dimes, then a cell phone. In another, a wrench and an envelope full of hundred dollar bills.

"Wow," he says, "I wonder who this belongs to."

He feels something small and hard at the bottom of a breast pocket and fishes it out. He holds it up to the light.

"A tooth," he says.

He sticks a finger in his mouth and works it around both rows of teeth.

"Hmm," he says, "not mine."

He's starting to feel uncomfortable. He reaches into the other breast pocket and pulls out a Polaroid photograph. It's a picture of three men standing on the porch of an old wooden building. One is smiling. The other two look confused. The smiling one looks familiar. He glances up into the mirror again.

"It's me," he shouts. "It's me!" He studies the picture more carefully. "I'm wearing these coveralls in the picture. They must be mine."

He clenches his jaw and purses his lips and burrows his gaze into the picture deeper and deeper. Sweat breaks out on his brow. He swims still deeper, through the eye that framed it, the camera that captured the light of it, into the darkness of the thing itself.

And he comes up for air, taking a deep breath and shouting, "I remember! I remember! Meatballs and Churchbells!"

The End

A guard raps on the door of Jimson's cell. There's no answer, so he enters. Jimson is sitting on the edge of his cot, looking down into the pages of an open book.

"Is it any good," asks the guard.

Jimson looks up at him. "I can't remember how it started," he says.

The guard nods. "Here are your clothes." He lays a stack of folded garments at the foot of the cot. Then he steps closer to Jimson, and leans down to whisper in his ear. "Our Comrade sends his condolences for the losses of your wife and daughter," he whispers. "If there were anything he could have done, he assures you, he would have."

Jimson stares into the book, unmoving.

"He has only two further requests of you," continues the guard, "and then you will be released from your service. First, you will don these clothes and accompany two other sleeper agents on a low security mission designed to help our Comrade defeat his adversaries in this sector."

Jimson begins to inspect the clothes lying beside him.

"When this first assignment is accomplished, we will provide you with a new identity, and you will begin your second assignment, a translation. This second assignment will be delivered to you at the place of your relocation. When the second assignment is complete, you will receive a reasonable pension and the freedom to live the rest of your life as you see fit, within the bounds of our initial agreement, of course."

"What's this for," says Jimson.

"It's a light weight Kevlar vest," says the guard. "It's not necessary, but, as you know, we value you, so please indulge us by wearing it under the coveralls. All necessary equipment for the first assignment can be found in the pockets of the coveralls."

Jimson rises and turns away from the guard. He stands looking up through the one high window of his cell for a long moment. A plane descends through the blue murk of the sky. He closes his eyes and inhales deeply of the antiseptic air of the institution. It smells like home now. The guard clears his throat, and Jimson turns quickly.

"Who are you," says Jimson.

The guard smiles. "I'm your guard," he says. "You've been in this prison for thirty-eight years. But don't worry. Today is your lucky day. Due to the recession and the decreasing value of government bonds, our budget's been slashed. We have to release twenty percent of our inmates, and you're one of the lucky ones. Change into these clothes, and I'll walk you to the bus stop. You'll know which bus to take."

Appendices

Appendix A

The following text is the transcription of a handwritten document I received shortly after I finished editing *Gnarly Wounds*. The envelope was postmarked February 8th, 2011, in Sibiu, Romania. I could find no return address on or in the package. Included in said package was a note which said simply, "Enclosed please find a translation of Nicu's prayer, found at the foot of a cliff." I here reproduce the full text, as it may be of interest to some readers:

"Yet another elder said: If you see a young monk by his own will climbing up into heaven, take him by the foot and throw him to the ground, because what he is doing is not good for him."

Verba Seniorum

Gravity, sweet gravity, you are all that we know
When we are high you bring us low
Praised be the fallen
May their descent never end
You lie us down in green pastures and think us through
You break us with the force of galaxies
The sun's salutation, the dinosaur's deep, the softness of nothing, the nothing of sleep
You are the strong and weak of it
You order us so simply our order is forever beyond us
You draw us through you like handkerchiefs through key holes
In all our laws lies the shape of you
And the shape of all things bears the likeness of you
You turn the turbines of my ears like the sea
We lie on our backs and look down into the sky and do not fall into it because of you

There is nothing like her which I can move away from which
you don't move towards me
Because of you there is no direction but what you speak
Time is the raiment you fill
Your voice a single vibration, a lifetime in length
You came to me in a heavy rain as I was running on the shore
of the sea
You came to me and you said to me, "You shall never escape
me
"I am as close as every atom of your being
"And I am farther than your farthest thought can know
"And I am all that you know
"And one day I will start over without you"
And I cried, "Why must you forsake me"
And you said, "Look
"Listen
"I am how you love
"And I am how you live"
And I cry, "I watch the weight lifters struggle with you
"There is nothing they can do to outweigh you"
"That is right," you say, "You die under your own weight
"Like rain on the face of the sea"
And you whisper, "Eat only that which doesn't sleep"
And you leave me
To lie in youb arms all night
I see the pendulum swing through you
And the stronger it resists, the faster it returns
You labor for all who listen
For you are will
Endless and incarnate
And we are wretched with pride
You lay down our arms
And we do not
You lay us down, out of trouble's way

And we stand

And we think we cannot measure you

Because we are the measure of you

I close my eyes and I open them and you have moved the world so the sun is in my room

How thoughtful without thinking

How could I have slept through such a journey as the sunlight has taken to me

You will bring me down from this mountain some day

As you bring down the waterfall

As you leave no trace but a wearing smooth of our homes

We fall through time and space to where we join the sea, or we turn and return to air again

I beg of you, if you must squeeze all trace of us from the world, tell me what I must do

What holy do you demand of me

Mystery of gravity

And in a drop of blood you tell me

"You must find a way out of me

"Or you must live the way you would want to live forever, so you might know what forever would be"

Gravity

What I thought was hate was you, and you made me great

What I thought was love was you, and you made me greater

You poured myth into me and made me a peer of the gods

You made every decision clear

You brought heaven near

You brought us together so strongly we emerged on the other side of you with new memory

You are the love that ends us endlessly

You are fertility

The soil itself is your seed

You are love and hate and I must remember this to find your living center

For your house of worship has no walls

For this valley is both empty and full with you

Come to me tonight and speak to me, for sleep is your sacrament

For in it we have submitted to you

As all that stands in you must balance, so too must all be weighed

Before it falls from mind to action

You feel it falling, but it never lands

For there are no forms but the densities you make, and we mistake

"Come to me," you order matter

"And I will make of you a fire enough to bring the void back to life"

Broken as a day lily under night's heel

I do not take my own life

For just the feel of you is greater than nothing

For the often oppressive weight of my limbs is your love, which I often forget

For to see blooming into you, like fireworks, our children

Before they fade from view

For simply to see your silhouette in the falling rain

For to fall with you into bed at the end of day

And feel through you the dark fire at the heart of the earth

Calling

For I too send you across all time and space

I am all directions in you

And all the world my house

Blessed be the falling

For there is no way to get to you but in the getting

No destination but in motion

For you are that which makes the stone too heavy for even its maker to lift

You are what labor is lost against

And you are what the lost labor against

And all energy is the radiance of your face

Blessed be the fallen, for they partake of your bounty

Redeem them in their drop

You are the terrible thought into which we turn

You are the heaven that burns in the heart of hell

You are the balance between vengeance and forgiveness

The constant between rise and fall

I fix my gaze on something, then slowly withdraw my sight from it, then slowly my thought from it, then: you

I stop the doors of the senses when I feel the weight of an ant: you

You are the taste of all I eat

You are what fills me

When I'm falling

When a moonless raining night is not present, I close my eyes and there, is you

I follow you to the center of the earth

And I open my eyes and you are there

And all faults disappear

Whenever my attention alights on a thing, at this very point, is you

I enter the sound of my name, and through it the sound of you

As I see many suns in water from one sun, I see from you, both bondage and freedom

They are words dissolved in you

There is a star, so far we shall never see it with our eyes

Yet through you I touch it instantly and always

It and I grow in each other's persuasion, as at the very center of me, where inhalation becomes exhalation, is you

As you tug at the tiniest mote of me, you hold the reigns of eternity

My form is what you draw upon, for you are the definition of all forms

As the earth is to the moon, my lover is to me

As circles flow into worlds and worlds into principles, you flow into me

And I swing in slowing invisible circles

For you are both knower and known

And we are how you remember

And we are what you forget

Until we hit rock bottom

Until we reach critical mass

Until you return us to the nothingness waiting patiently at the center of the expanding world

Remember us a moment before forgetting us again

Return us to the world in a flowering of flame

Appendix B

Shortly after I finished proofing the blue line of *Gnarly Wounds*, I received a postcard from Alba Iulia, Romania, postmarked December 1st, 2012. I hold it in my hand now. On one side is a sunwashed photograph of the statue of Mihai Viteazul on horseback, before Unification Hall. On the other is a message, written in a barely legible hand. It is signed simply "R." Again, I here reproduce the message for the benefit of readers who might find it meaningful. To date I have received no further messages pertaining to this book.

    Yours in Perpetuity,
    Jayson Iwen, Editor

"Every star in the firmament is a great eye through which I peer into you. For I live inside the flame that makes and unmakes you. Where I dance and creep the world comes to life in me. There is nothing without until I engulf it and release it from itself into being. I dance upon the bodies and trees and homes and books and art and garbage and all is one to me. It is I. Wherever I am I am, and all else is cold and dark and death and forever and ever. Amen. Let the ending begin. Again."

Acknowledgments

Ronald Ionescu, Jayson Iwen, and Nicholaus Iwinski would like to thank the following for their assistance with this one: Tom Barbash, Mark Bayer, Betty Anne Benes, Janet Bouche, Jovana Bouche, Zoia Ceausescu, Kayannda Davis, Michael Dumanis, Chad Faries, Judy Faulkner, Dara Fillmore, Chris Fink, Julie Gard, Lindsay Gatz, Jason Gitlin, Rita Grabowski, Chris Grimes, John Gunnon, William and Flora Hewlett, Ben Holmquist, Connie Horak, Bryan Iwen, William and Andrea Iwen, Dylan Jaconi, Anne Jamestown, Mike Jandl, Jason, Meatyard Johnson, Katie Lach, John McCormick, Emily Peterson, Kirk Peterson, Amanda Rilley, Michael Shaw, Bryan Tomasovich, Jamie White-Farnham, Maura Zephier, and Scott Zieher.

Emergency Press thanks Leah Rae Hunter, Frank Tomasovich, and Jill and Ernest Loesser for their generous support.

green
press
INITIATIVE

Emergency Press participates in the Green Press Initiative. The mission of the Green Press Initiative is to work with book and newspaper industry stakeholders to conserve natural resources, preserve endangered forests, reducd greenhouse gas emissions, and minimize impacts on indigenous communities.

Recent Books from Emergency Press

First Aide Medicine, by Nicholaus Patnaude

Farmer's Almanac, by Chris Fink

Stupid Children, by Lenore Zion

This Is What We Do, by Tom Hansen

Devangelical, by Erika Rae

Gentry, by Scott Zieher

Green Girl, by Kate Zambreno

Drive Me Out of My Mind, by Chad Faries

Strata, by Ewa Chrusciel

Various Men Who Knew Us as Girls, by Cris Mazza

Super, by Aaron Dietz

Slut Lullabies, by Gina Frangello

American Junkie, by Tom Hansen

EMERGENCY PRESS
emergencypress.org
info@emergencypress.org

Jayson Iwen is the author of two books, *A Momentary Jokebook* and *Six Trips in Two Directions*. He's studied and worked in software, security, insurance, construction, ecology, and education in a number of different countries, including the U.S., Cuba, Guatemala, Peru, Egypt, Syria, and Lebanon. He lives in Wisconsin.